# Seeking Forgiveness

# Seeking Forgiveness

Lea Rachel

Published by Writer's Design

First published in the United States of America
First edition printed in Saint Louis, MO, 2022


ISBN-13: 978-0-9908616-2-1
Library of Congress Control Number: 11342656551

Cover art by Stanislav Snihur

This book may be purchased in bulk for educational use.
Contact marketing@learachel.com
www.learachel.com

Writer's Design Press, St. Louis, MO

*Tomorrow is a possibility,*

*But if you love someone,*

*Tell them today.*

# Chapter 1

***I*** want him to know how sorry I am. I want to beg his forgiveness. For all I didn't understand, for all I never knew, for all I still have to learn. But the police have him and I can't reach him. My baby. My child. My son. Why am I hesitating to say it? To use the most obvious description? Because I generally gloss it over, try to act like it doesn't matter - why make everyone uncomfortable and bring it up? But it does matter. It is important. So here it is: My beautiful *Black* boy.

I married late. Thirty-four already when I met the man who appreciated my over-salted popcorn, my distracted housekeeping, my early 5:00 a.m. runs. I bumped into him in a bar, during happy hour, with half priced drinks and greasy appetizers that left misshaped oil puddles behind on the plate. He'd smiled, brushed off the long island iced tea I'd left behind on his shirt, as if liquid could simply be wiped off of linen. I'd smiled back, and within half an hour he'd rescued me from the all-male table of colleagues I'd been straining to have a conversation with.

I work at a bank and my co-workers are mostly puffy white men who shift their feet uncomfortably when I bring up stories about my son, Miles. Like the time Miles asked me why none of the comic books he brought home from the library had

Black superheroes in them. Miles was only six years old at the time and Black Panther hadn't yet made it to the movie screen. When my son mentioned the concept of a Black superhero, I'd literally been struck dumb by the notion. I'd stood in the middle of the kitchen with my hand on the refrigerator door and my mind spinning, trying to both picture the novel idea of a Black superhero for the first time, while also deriving a reasonable explanation for why my son hadn't yet seen one. The story as I told it to my colleagues was meant to be funny. I had meant it as, *Can you believe it? Had you even noticed that before? Who knew, but there are like no popular Black superheroes. I mean, in some books Hawkman is sketched a little darkly, but you can only pretend he's Black if you look at the pictures sideways. How dumb am I not to have noticed this before?* I had meant it as a revelation, like Wow! And wouldn't they share in the curiosity of my new discovery. But instead, most of my co-workers turned away at my stories, changed the subject, or most remarkably of all, got angry with me for bringing up irrelevant parenting stories.

The past sixteen years had been a lifetime of revelations about a world I hadn't known existed. And now it had culminated in this. My Black son, behind bars, alone, likely scared, possibly hurt, while I had to wait, impatient, angry, desperate, wishing I could make it all better, but not, at the moment, being enough for him. Had I ever been enough for him?

I remembered when I first researched adoption, thirty-five years old at that point and steeped in the knowledge that my eggs were antiquated and mostly dried up, like mini lima beans baked in the sun. I came across an article by a Black woman that told white women to stay away. *Black Children Need Black Mothers*, it was titled, and the essence of the argument was that white women should not even consider adopting Black children; that inter-racial adoption was, frankly, dangerous. At the time I was so stunned by the idea that someone would be against my adopting a child – a Black boy, for that matter, the child most likely to be left behind, looked over, passed by, left in the system until he'd aged out - that I thought I must be reading the article incorrectly. I must have missed something, an "and" or a "but" or some other qualifying contraction somewhere. I had to read the article two more times before I understood what the author was trying to say. White women simply don't have what it takes to raise a Black child in America.

I had assumed up until that point that adopting a marginalized child, saving a life from the system, giving a kid a home and a chance, was a good thing. Admittedly, it made me uncomfortable when friends I'd mention the idea to reacted as if adopting a Black child was profound and extraordinary (didn't people adopt babies all the time?), but at the same time, I never stopped them, never refused any accolades, never explored why it might be making me edgy to be praised for adopting a child. I had basked in the flattery of my mostly white friends, and entirely white family, as if my husband and I really were good people, about to do a great thing.

But then here was this Black woman, salt and pepper hair, large hoop earrings, earnest facial expression staring out at me from the computer screen, telling me to stay away from her kind. Informing me that, by definition, I would be a terrible mother for a Black child. My blood pressure ticked up as I reread the article and I thought, this woman doesn't even know me! If she only knew me, she'd see that my heart was in the right place. She'd understand that I mostly tried to do good.

But after the third reading I felt deflated, in large part because it offered no hope. The article implied that there was nothing my husband nor I could do to remedy the situation. We couldn't work to change the circumstances. We couldn't not be white. We could only stay away.

Up until that point I'd always prided myself on my work ethic. I was an A-type personality, determined, driven, resolute in my goals. I ran three miles a day, whether I was tired or not, I worked long hours at the bank until my evaluations rained down praise, I was even right this minute researching adoption like a conscientious person, trying to make a major life decision in an informed and thoughtful manner. Yet this very research was telling me that I was an inherently wrong person and that there was no way I could ever be right.

I realized later that it was the kind of message Black people had been hearing for years.

At the time, though, my reaction was to call an old high school friend from Detroit.

"Hey girlfriend," Tiffany purred, seeming happy to hear from me. Tiffany had been my best friend throughout my teenage years, and we'd spent countless hours on the phone in high school reassuring each other, supporting each other, trying to make sense of the world together. The sound of her voice was the sound of my past and her easy enthusiasm brightened my spirits. I asked Tiffany how her family was doing.

"They good, they good, you know, getting bigger all the time, especially Cedric." I laughed, recalling her husband Cedric's increasing waistline. We were all getting bigger, older, more seasoned.

It took me a minute, but I eventually brought the conversation around to the purpose of my call. "Nate and I have decided to, well, adopt. Through the foster system." There. I'd said it. I'd spit it out. In the moment of silence that landed between us my hands prickled with sweat. I imagined Tiffany responding, *Umm, why? Whatever gave you the idea that you could do that?*

But instead she squealed approval. "I'd stopped asking," she added, "because you got angry at me the last time I brought kids up. Even though, well, you aren't getting any younger." It was true, it'd been a rather long time since Tiffany and I had last spoken, and it was because I'd gotten sick of her always asking if I was going to have kids already. Just because so many of our friends had them, did that mean Nate and I had to too? Was it some kind of social obligation? What if I just didn't want to (though of course, I did)? I found out later that Tiffany kept bringing it up because she'd just wanted us to have kids around the same time, so our children could be friends. She hadn't been trying to pressure me, so much as share something with me.

"I know," I sighed. "I'm sorry. Well, we are looking into adoption now."

"That's great," she said supportively, giving me the space to go on.

"There's a lot of paperwork involved, it's crazy. You have to check what you're comfortable with, what you think you can and can't handle. The checklist is two pages long. Developmental problems, yes or no? Autism, yes or no? Drug exposure, yes or no? African American, yes or no?" Hearing myself say it out loud, I realized only then that 'African American' came in a list of options that were mostly negative.

"You can handle anything," Tiffany said, without hesitation. "You'll be a great mother, I know it. Just do it. And if it's a girl, remember to name her after me."

I smiled, recalling the time Tiffany had saved my life by pushing me out of the way of an oncoming school bus. She'd always been more aware of the world than I was; too often I stood oblivious, lost in thought. That belching yellow school bus had given me such a scare, however, that I'd promised to name my first child after her, something she'd never since let me forget.

"Thanks," I replied earnestly, "and you know it." And with that affirmation, I chose to assume that my closest Black friend had just told me it was ok to adopt a Black baby. I decided to move forward, and disregard the salt and pepper lady with the extra-large hoop earrings.

Looking around the waiting room at the police station sixteen years later, however, echoes of that long-ago article suddenly came back to me. A white mother will fail to teach a Black child his culture, it said. She will not understand his experience in the world, and he will grow up isolated, confused, and ill-prepared to protect himself in an America that will judge him harshly and do it's best to keep him down. A white mother *can not understand* what it means to be Black in this country, and so it is *dangerous* for a white woman to raise a Black child. It is unconscionable for her to even try.

Staring at the gray tile floor beneath my feet, at the brown cement walls of the unforgiving police station, I finally had to admit that the author had a point. I never should have adopted my son. I was not a good mother after all. I had indeed failed to protect my baby from this not unpredictable fate. He never should have been given to me in the first place.

# Chapter 2

*T*here was an evening, about five days after we'd brought Miles home from the hospital, where everything was perfect. I had just changed his diaper, fed him a bottle, swaddled him up tight, and brought his warm precious body close against my chest. His lips were pursed in a contented sleep, and I watched as his breath went in and out between them. I wanted to kiss them, but I refrained, afraid of waking Miles up. I sat in a rocking chair and sang softly to him instead, old lullabies that I knew my mother had sung to me.

My husband was still with us then. He hadn't left yet for the better job, the younger colleague, the easier life. He was still watching TV, beer in hand, a bag of Doritos splayed across his lap, when I'd gone downstairs later that evening. I had turned to him with Miles still in my arms and asked, "Can you believe this? That they just up and gave us a baby?" And we had both laughed, full-throated, from the gut. Miles had woken up then and gurgled along with us. Because if you thought about it, it was totally nuts that a stranger, with the blessing of a few officials and a mile of paperwork from the state, could just hand us a perfectly good baby and let us go home. Crazy.

But I was so, so glad that they had. Those first few months when Miles was a baby were blissful. I'm not saying that he didn't keep us up all night crying and making a fuss, I'm not saying that he didn't regularly get sick in my hair, or spill formula on the carpet, but the problems were simpler back then, more obvious, more easily correctable. I didn't have to guess what was wrong, or wonder if there were years of institutional history behind it. I didn't have to consider if his Blackness or my whiteness made any difference about what to do – he was just a baby and he was either hungry, tired, or cold. And I was just a mother, ready to help him.

Things started to change when we started going out of the house more with Miles by our side. There was a Starbucks a couple of blocks from our home, and one Sunday morning I convinced my husband (though he wasn't much of a coffee drinker) to get up and get dressed and walk with us to the coffee shop for lattes and early morning pastries. I tucked Miles into his brand-new stroller, braced him on either side with a few of the myriad, colorful stuffed animals that now populated our home, and walked through the neighborhood with my husband and child. We were a happy family, a unit, a threesome that was at last whole and complete.

It was a glorious morning. The sun was shining brightly, the summer air heavy but clear. Our neighborhood was middle class, with broken sidewalks and streets that needed repaving, but everyone took care with their own patch of lawn, as if insisting that better things were yet to come. I'd never had much of a green thumb myself, but I'd tried the first few years after we'd moved into our home to plant a few things and make our garden colorful. The rose bushes I'd carefully picked out from the nursery and planted deep in the soil had been eaten by rabbits, nearly to the roots. I tried hydrangeas next and they'd bloomed, but then disappeared as swiftly as they'd arrived. Magnolias were described to me by the arborist as easy going, as if they liked to stay out late and have a few drinks, but I found them to be recalcitrant, leaving the party early and never making another appearance. I planted a few more things but my heart was no longer in it. I took to apologizing to the bushes as I brought them home from the nursery, knowing they were likely going to die. After a delicate pink shrub made it through an entire year, but then withered away the next, I decided that a green lawn with no adornment was actually better. Neater. I kept on Nate to make sure it was mowed every two weeks.

As we neared the Starbucks I turned to my husband, who was looking straight ahead as if focusing on the finish line of a very distant race. His mood was always so inscrutable. I could never tell if the slight upturn of his mouth was a faint smile, or a sardonic smirk. He was my man of mystery, like all the fairytales described. Miles cooed and I bent over the stroller and cooed back, "Your first trip to Starbucks, it's an event!"

Strangers passed us on the sidewalk and I imagined them thinking, my, what a cute family, aren't they adorable? I looked for their smiles and appreciative head nods, like I always gave when I passed young families with newborn children on the street. So I was surprised when a middle-aged man in jogging shorts and Nike t-shirt glanced inside our stroller, and grimaced. He quickly turned his head to the side, as if he was only just taking the measure of the neighborhood around him, but he'd done a poor job of hiding the disgust that had momentarily stamped his features. Stunned, I stopped in my tracks.

"Did you see that?" I asked my husband, as the man swiftly moved past us.

But Nate refused to follow my gaze. "C'mon," he said after a moment. "I want to get back to make snacks for the game."

I wondered for a second if I'd seen what I thought I'd seen, but my husband's refusal to look me in the eye made me certain. I didn't know what else to say, so I pressed my lips together and walked on, not bothering to glance again at the jogger now well behind us. When my family got to the coffee shop no one cooed our baby, no one asked us how old he was, no one told us he was beautiful.

* * *

But I knew that Miles was beautiful. No one needed to tell me. And not just beautiful, but smart and sweet and surprisingly coordinated.

"Look at that," I exclaimed one afternoon, when Miles pulled himself up by the coffee table and toddled two steps forward. I glanced at Nate beside me on the couch, tapping away on his phone.

"That's great," he said distractedly.

Miles giggled and fell over and I went to him and picked him up. "Good job," I cooed, kissing my son's chubby cheeks. "You're practically walking!"

Within months Miles was careening around the house and following me from room to room. I'd park him in front of an Einstein video in the living room and go to fold laundry in the bedroom, but within minutes he'd have toddled to my side and gripped a hold of my leg with both arms. I'd swing forward, limping to the dresser with my son firmly attached to my leg, and we'd both devolve into laughter when he eventually fell off. When I made dinner in the evenings Miles bopped along beside me for a while, and then settled himself in the middle of the kitchen floor and observed my every move, like a concerned movie director. It was as if he knew he'd lost one mother already, and he was absolutely determined not to lose another.

"You smell so good," I told Miles after dinner one evening, bending over to kiss the top of his head. "Like pine," I kissed him again, "with maybe a hint of honey behind it."

"You compliment him too much," Nate said, walking by.

"Can you compliment a child too much?" I'd asked, surprised by the very notion.

"Of course you can. He'll start thinking he's king of the world, then he'll be spoiled, and then we'll have a brat to deal with."

For years I'd appreciated Nate's honesty and ability to help me focus on reality when I let my dreams and crazy ideas get the best of me. He'd counseled me on how to talk to my colleagues at the bank – how not to expect too much help from them, and how to instead offer my own assistance in a way that made them feel complimented and smart. It had worked wonders in that I'd gotten two raises and a promotion since I'd started taking Nate's advice. But this time, his advice just sounded mean.

"I've got to pee," I said, straightening up and walking towards the bathroom. Miles pushed himself up off the floor and followed me, clearly planning on heading into the bathroom with me.

"Isn't that a bit much?" Nate asked. "You look like a duck and her chick, but I don't think even ducks go to the bathroom together."

Perhaps I did indulge Miles too much. But truth be told, I adored the devotion. I treasured having someone need me so much they refused to let me out of their sight even for a bathroom break. "We're bonding," I called over my shoulder, and didn't draw the door to a close when I entered the bathroom.

That evening, when it was time for bed, Nate finally drew a line. "No," he said, stopping my hand when I pushed the covers aside to make room for Miles' tiny body in our bed. "Children shouldn't sleep with their parents."

So I went with Miles into his bright blue bedroom and stayed up with him until he fell asleep in my arms. Nate didn't seem to have a problem if I stayed up late into the night with Miles, I just had to do it in a sitting position, in the rocking chair in his bedroom, or on the couch in front of the TV. Miles simply couldn't enter our bed. Looking back, I've sometimes wondered if this was Nate's single feeble attempt at keeping our marriage alive; if it was his attempt to carve out a space for our love to deepen and grow, rather than wither and disappear as it eventually did.

* * *

Miles began talking in full sentences just after he turned two years old. He'd been saying a few words and phrases before then, *Mama*, *Dada*, and *tank you*, but I'll always remember the day he simply started talking.

We were on the floor of his bedroom and the sun was streaming into the room in patterns as the wind outside rustled the late summer leaves. We'd finished playing first with his red and blue trucks, then with his plastic phone that lit up and made astonishing noises, and finally with his Mega Bloks that snapped together in colorful towers. I'd wondered if it was time to take a nap, but instead pulled out the baby puzzles he'd just gotten for his birthday. "Let's try these," I said, and Miles nodded encouragingly.

There were two puzzles, a chunky alphabet one cut out of wood where the goal was to fit each letter to its place in the board, and a similar board puzzle, but with the cutouts being of various large trees. The alphabet puzzle had so many pieces I thought it might overwhelm Miles, so I tipped over the tree puzzle instead. Miles smiled as the pieces tumbled to the floor. I picked up a large green elm and slid it in its slot to show Miles how it was done. He picked up a weeping willow and worked to fit it in the bonsai's spot. His lips pouted in a frown, but he kept trying to fit the piece into the same incorrect slot. After a minute I reached over to help, and that's when Miles looked up at me and said with certainty, "No mommy, I do it."

I stopped perfectly still, withdrew my hand, and watched my son. The determined brow. The body bent over in concentration. The fingers that wouldn't stop moving.

He reminded me of my mother, committed to making a wrong right. A woman who'd volunteered with the homeless and knit countless blankets for the sick. He reminded me of my grandmother, brooking no failure. A woman who'd taught herself bookkeeping when my grandfather refused to let her attend college, and eventually landed a decent job. Miles looked up at me, and I smiled, recognizing the confidence in his clever wide eyes. He was clearly one of the family.

# Chapter 3

*I*t was two in the morning when I'd gotten the call that my son had been arrested. The proverbial single phone call. Luckily, I'd been awake to answer it. Usually that late at night I was asleep and my phone was in silent mode, but I'd happened to stay up late binge-watching Netflix, and when I'd realized Miles had missed curfew, I decided to keep watching until he came home. I'd remembered to turn the sound up on my phone after getting nachos from the kitchen.

I wasn't particularly worried at first. Miles had only missed curfew a few times before, and never by more than an hour, so I figured he'd be home soon. He just lost track of time, I thought, or got held up for some reason. It wasn't until my phone rang from an unspecified number, and I realized quite how late it was, that I sensed something might be wrong.

"Hullo," I answered, my voice scratchy from lack of use. I coughed to clear it.

"Mom, it's me. I'm-, I'm at the police station. Can you come get me?"

My heart beat so loudly I thought Miles might be able to hear it.

"They've made a mistake," he continued, "I didn't do anything wrong. It's- It's- Just come get me, ok?"

"Of course, ok," I said. "Are you al—", and the line went dead.

I threw a jacket on, grabbed the wrong purse, and rushed to my car. I didn't stop to think of what it might be helpful to bring, or who I should call to tell what was going on, I didn't think of anything but getting to the station. Our conversation had been so short; my son had told me practically nothing. Had he witnessed a robbery? Tried to break up a fight? Been in the wrong place at the wrong time? Well obviously he'd been in the wrong place at the wrong time, but how bad was it? Anything could have happened and as I drove to the station my mind bounced from one awful imagined scenario to another. I had to keep reminding myself that at least he was physically ok. He hadn't been involved in a deadly car accident. He hadn't been shot. I'd heard his voice on the phone, just minutes before. And from what I could tell, he seemed physically ok.

I drove into the police station and parked haphazardly in the uncrowded parking lot. Grabbing my purse, which I realized only then had nothing in it but my wallet – no Kleenex, no ibuprofen, no pen, no chap stick, none of the items I always needed the minute I didn't have them – I rushed into the building and strode up to the front desk, breathlessly asking to see my son. The reticent officer behind the partition yawned, and told me to have a seat. Somebody would be with me in a minute. I fought the urge to argue with him, to demand to see my son that very instant. Instead I swallowed, turned, and found a seat on the hard wooden bench in the middle of the waiting area.

A middle-aged woman with a large bosom and even larger purse sat across from me. Her face looked tired, her cheeks drawn. We glanced at each other for a second, and then she turned away and closed her eyes. When they didn't open again, I realized she was praying.

I closed my own eyes for a minute and thought about all the ways in which my son was a good person. How he picked up litter when we walked together in the park and always carried it, unasked, to a garbage can. How some of his very first words were *tank you* and *please*, and how he never failed to say them when asking for anything or if anyone did anything at all for him. How he gave hugs freely whenever he was asked, even past the age when most kids stopped giving their parents hugs in public.

Once, when Miles was five years old, we were walking in the neighborhood when we'd come across a little girl sitting on the curb, crying. Her red dress had bunched up in her lap and her skinny knees were sticking out vulnerably in front of her. I noticed a single puff of grass behind her legs, stuck in the nook where the curb met the street. Miles looked at me but I'd shrugged my shoulders, not knowing why the girl was crying. I tried to pull my son along but he'd let go my hand and walked up to her.

"Why are you crying?" Miles asked.

"My sister won't play with me," the girl replied, her pig-tails swinging from side to side. "No one will play with me."

Miles sat down on the curb next to her and offered her the toy he'd been carrying around all afternoon – a superhero figurine he'd only just gotten, and which he'd been coveting for months.

The yellow-haired girl looked at Miles, her tears no longer flowing. She reached a hand out and accepted the toy. They played together for twenty minutes before the girl stood and happily ran off. When my son returned to me I told him how proud I was of him for stopping, and making the effort to brighten the day of a stranger.

I looked down at my hands and my broken red fingernail polish. Miles was a better person than me in so many ways. We'd come across a homeless man once, asleep on the sidewalk just outside the doorway of a drug store downtown. It had been an incongruous sight, a grown man in his day clothes, boots and all, asleep on a couple of flattened cardboard boxes. My instinct had been to step around the body and simply keep walking, as with the girl crying on the curb. Miles' instinct was to stop, despite the smell, despite the oddity of a body in the middle of the sidewalk, and ask if the man was alright.

I continued to recount all the kind instincts that were inherent in my son; his generosity, his playfulness, his easy empathy. It occurred to me for a brief moment that most of these memories were from his early childhood, that since he'd become a teenager he'd grown aloof, abrupt, uncaring even, but I let those thoughts fly right out of my mind, like a mosquito that buzzes your ear, but then is quickly gone. The disciplinary calls he'd recently been getting from the high school I pushed even further from my mind.

Miles is a friendly, affectionate, misunderstood person, I told myself. He shouldn't be here. Whatever he was being accused of, there was no way it was true.

# Chapter 4

*A*fter that day with the puzzle when Miles was two years old, he never stopped talking. He'd tell me exactly what he wanted, "No banana momma, blueberries. I want blueberries." He'd tell me what he observed, "That lady has a big butt." He'd tell me how he felt, "Dada gone, I sad." Miles said this every time Nate disappeared into the basement. It made me sad too.

I'd always heard that girls were more verbal than boys; that boys talked as they got older, but even then, not very much. Miles, however, didn't fit this pattern. None of us ever seemed to fit any kind of traditional pattern, though, so I shouldn't have been surprised. I treasured Miles' chatter and eager voice. When I was away from home on a work trip or stuck in a late-night meeting, I begged Nate to have Miles call my phone and leave me voice messages. I never admitted to anyone how I saved every one of those messages, and listened to them over the years whenever I felt sad or mad. Even fifteen years later, Miles' baby voice cooing *Mama, where are you?* had the power to sooth my aching heart.

But Miles didn't just talk to me. He talked to strangers as well, men, women, children, adults, anyone who would engage him in conversation. Miles and I went to the corner Starbucks most Saturday mornings and spent a good hour there lounging in the oversized chairs, drinking coffee and orange juice and stuffing ourselves with muffins and croissants. If I got up to get a napkin or straw Miles would turn to whoever was closest and, whether they were alone or with a companion, ask them a question. "Do you drink coffee?" was his favorite, because it generally drew a laugh, but he'd also ask strangers if they were a mommy or a daddy, or if they drove a car. Not everyone responded to him kindly. Whether the other patrons didn't like being interrupted, didn't know how to talk to children, or just didn't have the time, many responded to Miles in curt, short sentences. For the most part, however, Miles was unfazed. It made me nervous all this reaching out that he did – I was an introvert by nature, and I'd never understood the value of small talk with strangers – but Miles relished these interactions, no matter how abbreviated they were. He was like a flickering flame, reaching out in all directions, seeking the current of oxygen that sustained his warmth. I would have expected most people to want to warm themselves by his adorable heat, but every once in a while he approached a stranger who didn't just lean back, but jumped away as if singed.

"Who told you it's ok to talk to strangers?"

Miles had apparently said something to an elderly woman with grey hair and buttoned up Burberry coat. I was still at the condiments counter, watching the interaction out of the corner of my eye, unaware of where it was headed or the negative tone it had already taken.

"Where's your mother?" The woman craned her neck and looked over Miles' head, scanning the seating area of the café. I was certain she wasn't trying to find someone who looked like me.

As I approached the two of them, I overheard the lady, bending forward towards my son, whisper, "Little nigger children shouldn't be left alone in here, unattended."

"Excuse me?" I practically yelled. The woman looked up, startled. Neighboring customers glanced our way. Miles seemed confused, his head tilted to the side. It dawned on me that my son had no idea what had just happened, or what kind of woman this was. I ran through my options – make a scene, but have my young, impressionable child see it and likely be affected by it, ignore what had just happened and smile and pretend the world was a safe place, even though it wasn't, try to talk to this woman like a reasonable person, though reason was never of importance in situations like this. I had a strong urge to slap this woman across the face, but my hands were filled with napkins and sugar packets and were shaking besides. I recalled my mother, who for years had funneled her frustrations and disappointments with the world into the red, blue, and yellow blankets she'd knit and donate to hospitals, loving care worked into every stitch.

I carefully placed the items in my hands onto our table and turned to the elderly woman. She was staring at me, her eyes wide and alert. I took a breath, but before I could say a word she grabbed her handbag, stood with a grunt, and strode out the door.

I sighed and sat shakily down.

"Why was she upset?" Miles asked.

I unwrapped Miles' muffin and handed it to him. He stuffed it into his mouth with both hands, not bothered in the least by the mess he was making.

"Not everyone is a good person," I finally said, smiling at him.

Miles nodded while continuing to eat with abandon. When he was done he looked at me, and I gave him my croissant as well.

"Why don't you just talk to me today?" I said.

"Ok," Miles replied, the happy light shining in his eyes again. I slumped in the chair then, feeling like I had dodged some sort of bullet. I made a mental note to research how, and when, to talk to a child about racism. And I kicked myself for not having done it sooner.

That evening when Nate returned home I told him what had happened. He'd been looking through the growing pile of mail on our kitchen counter and he paused, white envelope in hand, blue jacket still zipped up to the neck as if he might turn and leave again at any moment. "Are you really surprised?" he asked.

# Chapter 5

***I*** shifted on the hard wooden bench in the center of the waiting area, wondering what it was I was supposed to do to get my son out of jail. I looked down at my watch. It was now 3:12 a.m., about thirty-five minutes since I'd arrived at the police station, a little over an hour since I'd gotten the phone call. How long was one supposed to wait before being allowed to see a child in holding? Crime shows always skipped right past this waiting part. I wondered if it was obvious how out of my element I was, how anxious I felt wishing I knew what it was I was supposed to say or do. I looked around the waiting area, seeking some sort of human connection. Didn't anybody else think things were taking too long?

Besides myself and the still-praying-woman across from me, there were three other people in the station, two girls that looked to be in their early twenties, and an older man. The girls sat huddled together with their heads nearly touching, talking at a quiet but intense clip, their hands moving, their gum occasionally snapping. They were wearing very high heels that looked rather dangerous to me. I couldn't help it, I wondered if their mothers knew where they were.

The older man sat next to a small side table stamped with coffee rings. He was hunched over with his elbows on his knees, studiously cleaning dirt from beneath his fingernails. I wondered if he too was here for a son, or daughter. I coughed loudly, but didn't get his attention. Nobody, in fact, looked up when I coughed or cleared my throat or made any kind of noise whatsoever; we were all in our own little bubbles and nobody seemed in the mood for conversation with a stranger.

I stood, unable to help myself, and walked over again to the front desk. I rapped on the plastic partition that separated the police from the rest of us. The officer behind the barrier glanced at me, but didn't bother to come around to speak to me. He'd done it before, his expression told me, he wasn't going to do it again.

"Can I see my son yet?" I asked a bit too loudly. "Miles Zame? Miles Anthony Zame?"

"Still being processed," the officer said, without checking anything. He returned his attention to the computer screen in front of him.

A simmering rage boiled inside me. I stared at the bored-looking officer, trying to affect my frustration onto him with the steeliness of my gaze, but he ignored me. I wondered, yet again, what the magic words were to get him to get up and check on my son, but whatever they were, I didn't know them.

*Please help me*, a voice begged from deep within. But nobody heard it.

I sat back down and put my head in my hands. Most people called on family in times like these, but who could I call? Nate had been out of our lives for ten years at that point, and I doubted he would answer even if I did call. My parents were both gone, my only brother estranged. My thoughts turned to my cousin Chris, the only family member I could think of who had any history with the police.

Older than me by a few years, Chris was the cousin I'd idealized as a child. His family had lived a few blocks from ours, and on holidays we used to gather at his house, in their modest ranch filled with sports pennants and framed pictures of sailboats. His mom could be trusted to put out large piles of greasy finger foods.

I generally ended up following Chris around the house at such events, trailing him as he talked on the phone with his older, much cooler friends. The limited glances he threw my way were treasured signals I interpreted as meaning we were on the same team, the team that had to put up with these boring family gatherings.

In all the years of going over to Chris' house, however, I never grasped what was really going on. I heard stories of broken dinner plates and messes on the kitchen floor, but I hadn't understood at the time what they actually meant.

And then one day Chris disappeared. His parents got divorced and his mother moved with him to Texas, and like that, I no longer saw him. It was an abrupt loss, a painful loss I'd had no ability to process at the time. For years I only heard about Chris indirectly through the family grapevine, one aunt claiming that he was addicted to drugs, another mentioning that he'd dropped out of school, a third claiming he was wallowing under mountains of debt. It was never anything good anyone said about cousin Chris, and I heard less and less at all about him until one day, nearly three decades after he'd disappeared, he showed up at a family wedding.

I saw him standing alone at the bar, and after my initial shock had passed, I left my son on the dance floor and walked over to where he stood.

Chris smiled when he saw me and without hesitation lifted me up off the ground, in imitation of the hugs he'd given me when we were kids.

"It's good to see you," I said, close to tears though I couldn't have said why.

Chris offered me a drink and while we waited for it to be made we stood silently side by side, staring out at the dance floor.

"Is that your son?" he asked, pointing to Miles who was still toddling around to the music.

"Yes." I turned slightly and took in Chris' still handsome, if worn, older face. I tried to find in it evidence of what had happened, proof that whatever it was, he was all right now.

Our drinks came and Chris handed me mine saying, "It's got to be hard."

I looked at him quizzically, suddenly on my guard, afraid that my cousin was about to say something stupid and I'd have to reevaluate how much I'd always admired him. I didn't want to have to classify him as yet another of my obtuse relatives who didn't know how to handle me or my son, whose discomfort with us was obvious. I took a long sip of my long island iced tea. "What," I said, "being a mother?"

"No." Chris shook his head. "Having a Black son."

I put my drink down on the bar. My cousin's straightforwardness had confused me. No one in my family ever said what they were actually thinking. They made obtuse comments about having had a Black best friend in college, or watching the movie *Roots*, and I was supposed to infer from this that they were a "good person." But no one ever brought up Miles' race directly, as if it didn't exist, or weren't obvious, or weren't a profound and significant fact of our lives. I understood that talking about our interracial family made people uncomfortable, so I didn't bring it up, they didn't bring it up, it was never discussed, and instead this barrier remained upright between us. But Chris had never respected barriers of any kind, that was one of the reasons I'd always liked him.

"Sometimes," I admitted.

"I've long thought," he said, glancing at me before returning his gaze to the dance floor where Miles continued to giggle and squirm with abandon, "that if I'd been born Black, I'd be in prison right now."

I coughed and grasped for a napkin to cover my mouth. Chris leaned over and handed me one. After I'd recovered myself I stood on my tip toes and kissed my cousin on the cheek. "I've missed you," I said, wondering what had happened over the years to make my cousin so honest, so aware of the truths in life, instead of the lies we often told ourselves.

"I've missed you too, little cousin."

"Why'd you and your mom leave?" I suddenly asked. "What happened?"

"You don't know?"

I shook my head.

Chris smiled with one corner of his mouth. It was an attractive smile, but I saw the pain it masked. "I was arrested, for shoplifting." For a moment, all the negative things I'd heard about my cousin seemed to be true, but then, I knew there had to be more to the story.

"It was dumb, I shouldn't have done it, but I was mad at my dad for taking my Halloween candy. He found a way to punish me every single night, did you know that? If I looked at him wrong, no dinner. If I spoke before I was spoken to, a slap across the face. If I tried to watch TV on my mom's lap, I was told I was a baby and ordered to my room. I don't even remember why exactly he took my candy that year, but I do remember that I didn't get to eat even a single piece of it. After all that walking, after wearing that uncomfortable costume for hours, so much effort to earn it." Chris shook his head, still in disbelief. "So I snuck out of the house and went to the corner store – remember Naders?"

I nodded, remembering the corner store between our two houses, where we used to go to buy our gum and candy.

"Well I snuck off to Naders, but then when I got there I realized I didn't have any money. I was such a dumb kid." Chris squeezed his eyes with thumb and forefinger. "I was determined to have some candy though," he continued, "so I stuffed a bunch of Babe Ruths in my pants, not very well, and tried to walk out." Chris laughed. "No technique. I had no technique at all, man."

"I'm surprised old man Nader called the police. He always seemed so nice."

"He was nice. He didn't call the cops. He called my dad, and my dad did."

"But why—" I stopped, and started again. "How old were you?"

"Twelve. My mom wanted to just take me home, but my dad wouldn't let her. He insisted I spend the night in jail." Chris looked across the dance floor, remembering that night.

"My mom told me later that they fought about it all night, but in the end, my dad won. He always won."

Chris signaled for another drink, and I accepted another one too.

"It was the worst night of my life. That's all I'll say. Jail is not the place for a young boy. For any reason." Chris paused for a moment, and then continued. "When my mom came to pick me up in the morning, she already had our bags packed. And like that, we left." Chris turned to face me. "Can I offer you a piece of advice?"

I nodded.

"Should something ever happen to your son, never leave him in jail overnight. Anything could happen to him there. None of it any good."

It was as if Chris were speaking to me from the past; he'd already given me the advice I needed to hear. I closed my eyes now and tried not to think about what could happen to a small boy in a jail cell when no one was looking. *I'm trying*, I pleaded. *I swear, I'm trying.*

I never saw Chris again after that wedding. He died in a drunk driving accident the following year, his life never really recovered from his unhappy childhood and his early run-ins with the police. I pictured Chris' mother, her bouncy curls and round hazel eyes, and I thought about what she must have gone through. The heartbreak she must have felt unable, in the end, to save him.

# Chapter 6

*A*t least in the beginning Miles himself didn't much notice, or understand, incidents like what happened at the Starbucks. That started to change, however, when he entered preschool. I enrolled him in an academy near the bank where I worked, which was convenient for me, but I realized too late, not the best choice for my son. There were few other Black children at the preschool, and so Miles stood out, a chocolate brown swan in a bevy of bustling white feathers. And at four years old, the children were not shy about pointing out the difference. Two blond-haired, blue-eyed girls that looked to be sisters were particularly fascinated by Miles' skin and hair, and took to chasing him around the playground begging him to let them give him a bath. It wasn't malicious, I am pretty sure the girls honestly thought that Miles' skin was dark because it was dirty, and they didn't know any better because their parents had never talked to them about race.

A bigger problem was that none of the teachers seemed concerned. I discovered the dynamic with the other children when I went to pick Miles up early one afternoon, having gotten out of a work meeting ahead of schedule. I showed up to find Miles in a corner of the play area, building a city of wooden blocks all by himself. He was such a social child that this surprised me; I'd been sure I'd find him surrounded by at least two, three other kids. I'd pictured him laughing with friends, babbling incessantly as he always did at home. But Miles was by himself, not talking to anyone at all.

That's when I saw the sisters approach my son. They ran towards him laughing and squealing, waving small white towels in the air, and at their approach Miles bolted to the far corner of the room. I wondered at first if there might be some sort of flirtation going on, maybe a game whose rules I didn't comprehend, until I noticed that Miles was determined to stay hidden behind a wide plastic kitchen ensemble.

"Miles?" I called out, walking over to where my son crouched. "Sweetie? What's going on?"

My son jumped into my arms and gave me a hug much bigger than I'd been expecting. After a moment he peeked over his shoulder, looking to see if anyone had come up behind him.

"I saw you playing," I said. "Are those girls your friends?"

Miles shook his head, still uncharacteristically quiet.

"Tell momma what happened."

On the way home my son told me how the kids sometimes called him dirty. "Am I dirty?" he asked.

"Of course not," I snapped, my anger at the situation misdirected. I took a deep breath. "Did you tell your teacher, Miss M, about this?"

Miles nodded and looked out the window.

"Why do they call me black? I'm not black anyway," he said, "I'm brown."

I tried to explain that he was Black, but that it wasn't exactly about color, but about skin tone. But this only confused and upset Miles more, and admittedly, the more I talked about it the less sense it made. I was swimming in a murky swamp of definitional confusion with no notion of how to extricate myself. Miles insisted that if the other kids just understood that he wasn't actually black but *brown,* then everything would be fine.

I stopped talking, but my failure to agree with Miles made him angry.

"Why do I have to go there anyway?" he pouted.

"Because mommy and daddy have to work."

"I wish you didn't."

"Me too."

"Then don't."

"We have to, baby. We have to."

I knew I needed to address the situation at his preschool, but more than that, I needed to figure out how to make Miles proud to be Black. I wanted him to love his skin tone, not try to redefine it or explain it away as something he thought more palatable to others. How could I make my son embrace Black pride, when he had no example to go by?

* * *

The next day I cleared my morning schedule and took my son to preschool. When I parked in a non-temporary spot in the parking lot, as opposed to the usual fifteen minute drop off lane, my son noticed.

"Don't worry baby," I told him, "I'm just going to talk to Miss M for a minute."

The school was bustling by the time we got there at 8am. Children were playing in frenzied groups around drawing tables, Lego stands, and colorful buckets of balls and toys. The place was vibrant and alive; a sensory feast for the eyes and ears.

It took a few minutes for Miles' teacher to find the time to speak with me, but eventually she drew me to a small, adult sized table in a corner and we sat down.

"How can I help you," she asked, a hint of annoyance in her voice.

I shifted in my seat, then explained the situation, watching as her eyes drifted off to the side or over my shoulder. I wondered if she was even listening to me, as she was adding nothing to the conversation. Finally, she replied with the trite excuse that the children were just playing, that this wasn't about race, and that I shouldn't be making such a big deal over it. If I made light of it, I was told, Miles would too.

"Miles is such a sensitive boy," Miss M added, looking to me with a sly smile as if I'd agree with this shifting of the blame. "You can't give in to that." Everything would be fine, she seemed to imply, if I just didn't give in to his feelings.

My heart raced, and I could feel myself getting ready to ask Miss M if she actually cared about these children at all, when she surprised me with another question.

"What's his history, by the way?"

I stared at her. There wasn't a hint of embarrassment or hesitation in her manner.

"His history?" I pretended to have no idea what she was suggesting. Even close friends tended to ask me this question about Miles' origin with a bit more delicacy.

"Yes. Was he drug exposed? Because he's having trouble cutting with a pair of scissors. It's keeping him back from making crafts with the other children. We just want to know."

I was completely unprepared for this pivot in the conversation. My mind was still focused on the reason I'd come in this morning in the first place, I wasn't ready to talk about something else. Besides, I sensed some sort of accusation in the woman's voice, and she was really starting to piss me off.

I took a deep breath and squeezed my hands together under the table. I knew that knowing my son's past would make little difference in helping him in the present, so I said nothing. I just stared at Miss M and shrugged, refusing to confirm or deny her preconceptions. I refused to give her the satisfaction of pigeonholing my son, and I enjoyed watching her growing annoyance at my continued silence.

The meeting ended in a draw. Miss M assured me she'd watch the girls, but I knew that she wouldn't. I assured her that I'd practice using scissors with Miles at home, but we both knew I wouldn't. I never had to. I found out soon afterwards that Miles was simply left-handed. Miss M had been trying to make him cut with a pair of scissors that were made for 'normal,' right-handed children, and he was having difficulty because he was left-handed. Unfortunately, by the time this was figured out my son had lost interest in arts and crafts of any kind. He'd been reprimanded by the preschool teachers enough at that point that he thought he couldn't do it, wasn't any good at it, and though I'd encourage him and buy him stacks of coloring books and pastel-colored paper, he'd just shake his head and turn away from anything having to do with glue or scissors.

This was just one episode, of many, that as I got older and more experienced I wished I'd handled differently. Looking back on it nights when I couldn't sleep – after I'd fought with Miles yet again as he grew older and bigger and angrier - I'd think back and wish I'd had the presence of mind and grace of spirit to ask Miss M, in a calm but straight-forward manner, "Why would you assume that he was drug exposed? Because he's Black?" If I'd asked that quick-to-judge woman such a point-blank question, what, I often wondered, would she have said? And would it have made any difference for my son anyway?

# Chapter 7

*A*t 3:38 a.m. the glass partition slid open and an officer called out a name. The two women in high heels I'd noticed earlier stood and walked forward together, their shoulders touching, their hands nearly clasped. I felt a surge of jealousy for their obvious friendship. I hadn't had anyone stand by my side like that in years. In high school Tiffany and I were that close. And for a couple of years early in our marriage Nate and I were. But it'd been a long time since I'd had a friend to hold hands with.

Miles was my support system now. And when he wanted to, he was great at it. Just a few weeks before he'd comforted me at the end of a terrible day where I'd made a mistake in front of my boss, had a near car accident on the way home, and then spilled wine on my favorite blouse at dinner. All relatively minor upsets in the scheme of things, but compounded together in a single day they had left me battered and unmoored. I'd been standing in front of the kitchen sink, drenched in water as I scrubbed my blouse, when Miles had rebalanced me. He'd come up next to me and just started talking, telling me about the experiment he'd done in science class that day, about the book he was reading in English, about his Fortnite account and the latest skin in the item shop. It wasn't a conversation so much as Miles sharing pieces of himself, and those pieces clicking together into a delicate buttress that kept me upright. He knew how much I treasured his stories, and he didn't always share them with me now that he was a teenager. But that day he did, and I closed my eyes recalling the past comfort of his presence.

A phone buzzed loudly in the police station, startling everyone in the room. I locked eyes with the woman across from me, but we both shrugged, neither of us knowing whose phone it was.

"Shit," the girl standing closest to me said, "that's mine."

"Don't get it," her friend said.

"You know I have to." She fumbled through her purse and brought out a rhinestone encrusted iPhone. As she cupped it to her ear her long brown hair cascaded over her shoulder like a waterfall. "I know," she said, annoyance clipping her voice, "yes, I know." She turned then and angled her body away from the police partition and more towards me. In a quieter voice she continued, "but you don't understand. We didn't have a choice. No, that's not right— We tried. We—"

I could hear a deep, authoritative cadence on the other end of the line. The girl shifted her weight, glanced at her friend, and then her gaze landed on me. I smiled, trying to appear friendly, wanting her to understand that I knew what she was going through. She stared at me for a second, then rolled her eyes and turned away. It was the same sort of dismissive gesture that had become common with Miles over the past year and a half.

"Don't you walk away from me," I yelled at Miles not that long ago.

"Whatever, Mom."

"This conversation isn't over. Get back here right now."

"You can't order me around. I'm not your slave. You can't just tell me what to do, and all up in a second, expect me to do it."

"That's exactly what I can do. I am your mother."

"And a terrible one at that."

Miles had hit the nail on the head, and it had gone in deep.

I'd stood there speechless, wondering how we'd gotten to that point. Wondering when our relationship had devolved into a constant argument that seemed both endless and unfathomable. Where was the moment when things had gotten so far off track?

I had wondered it then, and I was still wondering it now.

I'd righted our ship from a misdirected course once, years ago, when I'd pulled Miles from that awful preschool with the ignorant Mrs. M. It had taken effort, locating a new preschool where Miles would actually fit in. Where Black families and white families and Black-and-white families like ours all came together and didn't have a problem with it. I had had to spend hours researching facilities on the computer, and then days driving around St. Louis to preschools far from our home, poking around during operating hours to see if they were actually diverse (as opposed to just the pictures they displayed on their websites), if they offered quality educational programs, were reasonably clean, and fully staffed. A surprising number were not. But at last, in his final six months before kindergarten, in that last year we could still call ourselves a family of three, Miles went to a school where he belonged.

And he flourished there. I hadn't realized the extent to which he wasn't flourishing before, until I saw the progress at his new school. Miles learned to write his name within weeks, and came home bearing large pieces of paper with M I L E S rendered in bold green crayon. He developed the ability to keep a beat on a djembe and quickly gained a fascination with music and instruments of all kinds. His creativity in so many areas exploded.

One afternoon I went to pick Miles up from the preschool and found him building a city out of Lego with two other children. They'd made a model of the street the school itself was on, including the gas station on the corner, the office building next door, and the large garden and playground out back. I bent to look admiringly at the little desks with computers on them in the office building, the trucks with drivers in the gas station, and the swing sets in the mini Lego playground. The children had even made rows of bushes in the garden, where they'd been learning about planting seeds and growing vegetables.

"What will these be?" I asked with delight, pointing to the tiny green plastic leaves.

"Vegedables," Miles confirmed.

I noticed at the end of the build the rectangular outline of something new being constructed. "What's that going to be?" I asked.

"A liberry."

I tried to recall seeing a library somewhere on this street, but couldn't. "A library?"

"For you," my son said. "Because you love books."

I blinked.

"It going to be blue," he continued, "your favorite color."

As the days passed the Lego city grew in complexity. More minifigures were added, including workers in chairs with pencils in their hands, teachers in the playground with megaphones and clipboards, even an attendant at the gas station in hat and uniform. Miles would come home and we would talk about the build as I made dinner, imagining the things he could add to it, sometimes going through our own Lego pieces to see what might work as a sign post or a revolving door. Miles asked Nate to join him once, but when he said no, Miles didn't ask again.

As the months rolled by Nate spent more and more time in the basement, if he came home at all. I knew that things weren't good between us, that we needed to work out some disagreements over money and issues with the house, but I maintained the delusion that we were just in some sort of a phase; that couples had ups and downs and while the troughs could get pretty low at times, inevitably there would come an upswing.

By the end of summer, however, I had started to sense that it was more than a phase. I woke up one morning in August without Nate by my side and had the feeling like you get on a hike, when after a bright and sunny start you turn around, the cold wind whipping your hair and shirt, and realize that the horizon behind you has gone dark.

"Where were you?" I gathered the courage to ask Nate one evening, when he finally showed up as Miles and I were eating dinner. It had been so unexpected, his appearance that night, that Miles and I both stopped chewing mid-bite to stare as the back door opened and he entered the kitchen.

Nate struggled with a response. After a minute he gave up and shrugged his shoulders. "Out."

It was such a trite, uninformative answer I found myself laughing. I laughed so hard my sides hurt, and then as Nate gathered his things and kissed Miles on the top of the head before leaving again, I started to cry.

I felt like a failure. That's what no one tells you – divorce is so common nowadays you think before it happens to you that it's no big deal, that it's just another familiar, if unfortunate, inconvenience, like a root canal – but it's so much more personal than that. When someone leaves you who you thought would be by your side forever, who you thought had made a promise to stay with you, who you assumed would put in the effort, it's a betrayal of the bitterest kind. And you can't help but wonder what you did to deserve it. It felt as if someone had pulled the plug on my life, and both the electricity and the light had gone out.

I could sense Miles by my side and I looked up from my crying. I knew I needed to pull myself together for my son. Miles was patting my back, like I always patted his when he was sick or sad.

"Momma," he said softly.

"Yes baby," I replied, drying my eyes with the bottom of my t-shirt. Miles was holding his hand out in a fist.

I looked at it, confused, until I realized that he wanted to give me something. I reached my hand out to his and my son opened his palm over my own. His fingertips grazed my skin and I felt a Lego minifigure drop into my grip.

I looked down at the figurine, straight brown hair, round dark glasses, short skirt, a determined expression on her face. She looked remarkably like me.

"It's you," my son confirmed, "and she's got your favorite things – coffee and a book." The minifigure was indeed holding a little square book in one hand, and a round red mug in the other.

I was wide-eyed at the likeness. I turned the minifigure over in my hands. "It's perfect."

"I keep it with me," Miles said, as if admitting a secret. "In my pocket. At the other school, I'd bring it every day, and hold on to it."

"You brought this to school, every day?" How did I miss that, I wondered. How did he not lose it, or have it confiscated by the teachers?

"Yes, but you need it more now."

"Thank you," I said hoarsely, taking the Lego figurine from my son and wiping away my tears.

That minifigure became a sort of talisman between my son and I. When he had a bad day at school or a hard time sleeping at night, I'd slip it into his coat pocket for him to find later when he needed it. Miles would keep it for a few days and then, when I seemed particularly sad, usually after another argument with Nate, I'd go to my room and find it nestled on the pillow of my bed. We quietly passed it back and forth between us, never admitting anything out loud, never having to. It was just a Lego minifigure passed between mother and son, a reminder that we were loved, that someone was paying attention.

"Ok," the girl said, ending the call and putting her phone back in her purse. When she straightened up she glanced my way again, and this time, she smiled.

# Chapter 8

*A* lock clicked and everyone in the waiting area looked up as the door next to the police partition at the front of the room opened. A woman walked out, escorted by a tall policeman. Her two friends quickly joined her and the three of them all stood together, hugging and talking. I watched as one of the women tucked the hair of her reunited friend behind her ear. It was such an intimate gesture I had to look away. Ten minutes later they were gone and the police station felt more desolate than ever.

A feeling of loss gnawed at me. It was similar to the loss I'd felt after Nate had left, only this time, it wasn't as if someone had unplugged my world to make it go dark, it was more like they'd taken a torch to it and burned everything to the ground. What was left was a charred emptiness, and a vibrating heat that made me unable to sit still. I stood, walked to the window at the far end of the waiting area, then turned and sat back down again.

If Miles' father were here, I wondered, would he be of any help right now? Either the father I tried to give him, or the one that was of his blood? We never found out who Miles' birth father was, his birth mother having declined to tell us at first, and then dying before she could tell us. I used to sometimes imagine his birth father showing up in our lives, tall, strapping, reflecting an older version of my handsome boy. When the doorbell rang it would be a surprise, a miracle reunion like you saw could happen on daytime TV. Or, maybe Miles' birth father would show up at my work, bearing flowers and regret and courting me, as well as my son, and telling us both how he had been looking for us for years. Or maybe, just maybe, he would show up now, burst through the door of this horrid station, drawn somehow by the biological tug of a son in need, and rescue us from this nightmare that seemed to be taking forever.

I knew my ex-husband would never show up. I knew it would be useless to contact him, though he spent the first few years of Miles' life with us, and Miles still recalled him as something of a father figure. Nate hadn't been a bad father, really, but if I were honest with myself, he'd never been a willing one either. I'd dragged him through the motions of fatherhood, first the adoption classes, then the lessons on swaddling and feeding, while he'd stood woodenly by, nodding, his attention always elsewhere. After Miles was born, Nate tried, but less and less over time, reaching for the TV remote instead of his son, finding other outlets for his passions. When the divorce papers arrived in the mail I'd sat down and finally admitted that I'd layered my hopes upon him, like thin coats of varnish, hoping they'd build up to something shiny and durable, when in fact all they had done was dull and suffocate the person beneath. Nate couldn't breathe, and so he had left us.

I brushed the memory of my ex-husband from my mind. It hurt too much. I thought about my brother, Sam, who I'd been close to once. Sam was older than me by two years, and we'd been friends growing up. He had protected me from the mean kids on our block when I was little, and as I grew up he let me hang with his friends when they came over. He never made me feel unwanted and, indeed, as I got older his friends even seemed to enjoy having me around; they liked seeing how I reacted to a dirty joke, or a can of beer. By the time Sam and I were both in high school I'd been introduced not just to beer and cigarettes with my brother and his friends, but to pot and acid as well. I'd always thought it was so chill of Sam to include me in his circle. It only got awkward when his friends asked me to buy from the dealer for them and I refused.

But after high school, Sam and I drifted apart. We had other interests, other worlds, and Sam left St. Louis, hopping around the Midwest before settling not all that far away, across the river, in Illinois. He ended up in a well-kept suburb about an hour's drive east, and when Miles was small he visited a few times. After Nate left and Sam heard about it, he called and asked if we needed anything, offering more often than before to come over and see us. It was the familial help I'd always hoped for. Sam would arrive bearing cookies and milk – he insisted that children needed lots of milk to grow – and sit with Miles and talk to him, interrupting the games they sometimes played to take selfies with his smiling nephew. I discovered later, after his calls and visits abruptly stopped, that he'd been using those photos to impress his boss at work; he'd been angling for a promotion from a lead manager that was Black, and he thought his Black nephew would win him points. Sam's visits pretty much stopped when the promotion fell through.

I shifted uncomfortably in my seat and realized that I needed to *do* something already. I needed to act. We didn't need a father, husband, or brother, but a lawyer. A well-paid lawyer that would wipe the smirk off those police officers' faces behind the front desk.

I hesitated for a little while longer, but as far as I could tell there was no movement on Miles' case and I was sick with worry. If I was handling this so poorly, I thought, what was Miles going through? How was he holding up? I did my best not to imagine it, not to picture the dark cell Miles might be sitting in, not to see the harsh tactics the police might be using on him, not to think about his hunger, his cold, his distress.

I didn't want to do it. I really didn't want to make the first move, but I took out my phone and stared at it. I looked up my uncle's phone number. My uncle was a well-paid lawyer. My uncle had contacts. My uncle would know what to do.

But my uncle was also a bigot.

Uncle Ian was my mother's brother, and though from the same gene pool as her, he had turned out unlike her in nearly every way. He was my proof that blood didn't matter, that people could turn out to be anything, that genetics predicted so little.

When I'd first announced to the family that Nate and I were adopting an African American child, Uncle Ian's response had been to storm from the room. It was the Thanksgiving holiday and we were stuck in a house together for the whole of the afternoon, but Ian was more than prepared to make the day uncomfortable for everyone who'd unwittingly shown up. By the end of that afternoon, he'd loudly argued with me over the shooting of Trayvon Martin, the iniquities of Affirmative Action, and the color of Barack Obama's skin. He insisted that Obama wasn't Black.

"Obama isn't Black?" I'd echoed in disbelief.

"No. Obama isn't Black, because he didn't grow up in the streets. I read his autobiography," Uncle Ian stated with misplaced pride. "You aren't Black if you don't grow up playing in the streets, dirty and shoeless."

"Ok, so," I stammered, "your argument is that because Obama wore shoes as a child, his skin today can't be considered Black?"

"Essentially."

I stared at my uncle's confident grin, the look that implied that what he'd said made perfect sense, the swagger indicating his assurance that he'd actually proven something. I could think of nothing good to say in response. I'd made Nate get up at that point and leave, even though he'd been hoping for a second piece of pecan pie.

I shuddered recalling all of the mean and hurtful things Uncle Ian had said to me over the years before I'd finally cut off contact with him.

Did it count as white privilege, I wondered, if I had to use a racist relative to get my Black son out of jail?

I stared at Uncle Ian's phone number for another minute, then I stood and walked outside the police station for some privacy.

I didn't know if my uncle would even answer a call from me. But I was Miles's mother, and this is what a mother did. She did whatever she had to, to help her child. I took a deep breath of the cool night air, and pressed dial.

# Chapter 9

***O***f course, my uncle would want to know what had happened. But where to begin? We hadn't spoken in years, and he didn't know much about the details of Miles' childhood, not about the reasons for Nate leaving, not about the solitary years afterwards, not about the troubles we'd had trying to find a neighborhood where we fit in as an inter-racial, single mother, adopted son family. Did the trouble start with kindergarten? When I tried to enroll Miles in a school that was both academically strong and reasonably diverse? I'd had no idea, at first, how rare that combination was.

Just before Miles turned five, I'd dutifully gone to the elementary school near our new apartment for an open house for enrolling parents. I'd felt heavy with the sadness of Nate's absence for such a milestone, but as I grabbed my favorite black skirt and fitted blue blouse from the closet, I'd also felt I could handle it. I bolstered my confidence by also wearing the button rose earrings my grandmother had given me just before she died. They were delicate looking, with thin red-gold swirls, and my grandmother had told me she'd worn them at her very first job interview, and at every interview after that until she'd landed a bookkeeping job. They were slow acting, she had told me, but they always came through in the end.

I'd entered the school with a number of other mothers (and one father), and sat down in the library for an informative talk about everything the school had to offer. As the assistant principal droned on, I reached over from my seat and pulled a book from the child-sized bookshelf next to me. I turned the pages and was surprised to find many of them torn, the last few missing. During the head principal's turn at the lectern, the bulb on the projector went out and everyone laughed as a joke was made about the importance of improvisation.

Next, we were given a tour of the classrooms. Square spaces with square desks, few windows, and no computers. I raised my hand to ask where the computers were, and was told that the four working machines were reserved for individual check-out. Four working computers? For the entire school?

The combined art/music room was in the basement. The cafeteria next to it, offering a lingering fetid odor, had a linoleum floor that stuck to the bottom of everyone's shoes. Outside, the small playground was filled with dilapidated, rough metal equipment that looked many years too old. For the first time, I began to doubt my choice of neighborhood.

I'd convinced myself since we'd moved in a couple of months earlier that where we lived was a great neighborhood for Miles and I. We didn't live in the so-called "best" part of town, where the wealthier people lived, but we lived in a good part of town, and what I meant by that was not just the affordable rents and the nearby expressway arteries, but the mix of people from so many different walks of life who'd also chosen to settle there. Miles didn't have to feel like the only Black kid on the block, and where we lived there weren't just Black families and white families, but immigrant families from all over the world, and even a few inter-racial families that looked vaguely like ours. It was all very cosmopolitan.

But what I'd convinced myself was cosmopolitan, I had to admit while touring the local elementary school, could also just be called poor. We now lived in a poor neighborhood, with poor resources, and the local schools reflected it.

I worried over it for the next few weeks as the school year approached, but in the end, decided to stay put. We'd give the local public school a try. I'd done further research and come to realize that there was no ideal school for my son anywhere, in all of St. Louis. A school that was both highly rated academically *and* majority Black simply did not exist, and it was my ignorance to have thought that there would be one, and I just had to find it. After hours of investigation into the educational system in America, I eventually understood that I had to choose between a strong school academically, *or*, a majority Black school where Miles wouldn't feel out of place, but I couldn't have both. Deciding which one was better for my son was a next to impossible task.

At the time, I talked it over with Tiffany. I found out that she had gone through the exact same agonizing decision herself only a few years before. In the end, she'd decided to move to a nearly all white part of town; she'd chosen academics over diversity.

"But why?" I asked.

"You know Sayid's going to be a lawyer or doctor, right?"

"Sure," I laughed out loud, "of course."

"Well if he's going to be a famous surgeon, first and foremost," she said confidently, "he needs a good education. Like, top of the line."

"Uh-huh."

"He can get his Black culture from us, at home, from my mother especially – she's never gonna let him forget who he is."

"No, no she most definitely is not."

"Besides," Tiffany continued, "being surrounded by whites all day is actually a good thing. If Sayid's going to be a top doctor or lawyer, he may as well learn how to navigate a world with mostly white colleagues early. If he's going to need to figure out how to be the token Black in a room, he may as well do it when he's young."

Tiffany's argument was sound, but depressing, as I couldn't make the same choice. If I stuck Miles in an all-white school, he'd also come home to an all-white family, and how out-of-place would that make him feel? He might think he didn't fit in, anywhere.

I'd always loved school, I'd been an A student, had enjoyed impressing my teachers and learning new things. It broke my heart to think that Miles might feel out of place at school, and not want to be there. It was a difficult decision but I decided, in the end, that I wanted my son to feel comfortable in the world without me, I wanted him to *like* going to school, and so I chose diversity over academics, unlike Tiffany. Besides, I told myself, like Tiffany I could add the missing element when he came home. I could bring the extra academics that were missing at school to Miles' home life. I pictured us doing loads of homework together every night at the kitchen table, like my own mother and I had done. What I couldn't automatically add to Miles' life, was color. So for us, the best decision was to stay where we were and support the local school. I'd just have to make the extra effort at home to make sure Miles was on top of what he needed to learn.

It turned out to be the wrong decision. A single working parent can not rescue a child from the effects of a failing school district. I was not superhuman, I didn't have superhuman reserves of time or energy, and I needed a school that worked with me, instead of mostly against me. When I had questions about Miles's homework and what he was supposed to be learning, the teachers didn't return my calls. When I made inquiries as to whether there were extra resources to help Miles with math, his most difficult subject, I was told that the district had no money for extra resources, unlike the schools where my colleagues from the bank sent their children. If Miles was failing, we were entirely on our own. The school administrators seemed more annoyed, than grateful, that I cared about my son's performance at all. By second grade Miles's teachers had given up on him, and relegated him to the back of the classroom, where they could more easily ignore him and his energetic outbursts.

But what was perhaps worse, and certainly more unexpected, was how my son was treated by the other children. After witnessing me pick him up from after-care one day, the children at Miles' school started calling him orphan-boy. I found out when my son asked me during dinner one evening what an orphan was.

"Did you say *orphan*?"

"Or-fen," Miles said with emphasis, distaste in his expression.

"Is that on your vocabulary list this week?" I asked with wonder, putting my fork down to think about how to define the word. It wasn't the first time the school had put a difficult, obscure word on his vocabulary list. I charitably assumed there was some phonetic reason for it, like learning it helped his verbal motor skills, or some such thing.

"Orphan's an old word, really," I expounded. "You don't hear it much anymore. One of my favorite authors used to write about orphans, Charles Dickens, he was a British author who wrote more than a hundred years ago. But I'm getting off topic," I laughed, swallowing the remainder of my wine. I wondered if it might not be a bad idea to read *Oliver Twist* as our next book together before bed. "An orphan is a child who has lost both of his or her parents," I continued. "In the old days, such children would go to live in a special home, called an orphanage." As I talked I sensed the dangerous territory I was entering. "But we don't have orphanages anymore. They're a thing of the past."

"How does someone lose both their parents?" Miles asked, not looking at me.

"Well, to be honest, it can happen for a number of reasons. A car accident, sickness, maybe the mother dies in childbirth and the father another way..." I found myself rambling on about frightening things that could kill people, not sure how to re-orient the conversation.

"Am I an orphan?" Miles asked when I finally stopped talking.

For a moment, the world stood still. I heard the ticking of the clock in the kitchen, felt the sweat prick underneath my arms, saw the wetness edge Miles' eyes.

I shook my head and gathered my son into my arms.

"No," I told him, "you are most definitely *not* an orphan. I am your mother. And you have a father, even if he isn't around right now." I wanted to kick Nate all over again for leaving us, for leaving Miles vulnerable to these thoughts of abandonment. "Why would you think you were an orphan?"

Miles told me then about the boys at school who assumed that his "real" parents were gone, because I couldn't be his "real" mother. I was white and he was Black and we didn't match and that meant something was wrong, most definitely not right.

I kissed Miles on the top of his head and brushed away his tears. I was his mother, I assured him, and that was never going to change. Ever. Those boys just didn't know what they were talking about.

We sat together in silence for a bit, then I quietly asked, "Do you want to talk about Sharelle?" Sharelle was Miles' birth mother. I brought her up whenever I could. I didn't want Miles to ever think he couldn't ask me about her; I didn't want him to ever assume his past was something we couldn't talk about, or worse, something to be ashamed of.

But Miles shook his head. "What if you leave too?" he asked instead.

It took every ounce of effort I had in me not to cry at that moment along with Miles. But I needed to portray strength. Miles couldn't see me sad or weak or confused about this. I had to reassure him in no uncertain terms that I was never going to leave him.

I looked my son in the eye and told him that he was the most important thing in my world and that I would never, ever leave him. I then told him that he needed to correct those boys; he needed to tell them that he was not an orphan. I retold Miles all the stories from his past that he loved to hear, about how he had peed on me the first time I changed his diaper in the hospital, about the time he drew all over the kitchen walls with red and blue crayon, about how he used to dance around the living room in nothing but a Tupperware bowl on his head and a diaper on his behind. He laughed a little then, and snuggled deeper into my arms. He asked if he could sleep with me that night in the big bed – a treat I usually said no to – and I hugged him and said, of course.

The next afternoon, the bullies at the school punched my son in the face when he let his guard down and told them about the Tupperware bowl, and I had to rush from work to pick him up from the nurse's office. Safe in our apartment I held Miles close, kissed his bruises, and changed the band-aid on his chin. I had no good explanation to give him for what had happened. But I vowed that day to find us a new apartment, in an entirely different neighborhood. At the time I had hoped it would be enough to turn our fortunes around. At the time, I thought I was protecting him.

Ten years later, standing outside a police station, I wondered if it had ever been possible to protect my Black son. I was searching for a moment when our fortunes had diverged, when some event had happened to lead us down this darkened road we now seemed to be on. But increasingly, I had the feeling that there was no singular event that starkly divided our path from a sunny and innocent stroll, into a dark and divergent woods. History had laid this trail down before us, and like babes, we were blindly walking down it.

# Chapter 10

*T*he phone rang with no answer from my uncle, so I ended the call and slipped the phone into my back pocket. The evening air was cool and refreshing and I breathed it in. I stared out at the gray horizon beyond the station and wondered what my own mother would do if she were here with me, what she would say to comfort me. She'd always been good at saying the right thing to make me feel better about myself – when a boy I liked didn't like me, or I failed to make a sports team at school – my mother had the perfect quip to make me believe that they were the ones who'd lost out, not me.

When I was nine years old my mother and I had rescued a kitten from the side of the road. He was scared, pressed up into the corner of a cardboard box that had a sign on the front that read: Free Kittens. By the time we stopped to look inside the box, there was only one kitten left, cold and alone, his siblings all taken from him. I had reached my hand inside the box to pet him, and the kitten had scrunched himself even further into the corner, as if through sheer effort he could meld his body into the cardboard. I could still remember the sound of the other cars as they whizzed past us on the road, not pausing to slow down even a little bit.

*You'll make a great mom one day*, my mother had told me, watching me take care of the tiny kitten once we'd brought him home. At the time, I'd looked at her as if she'd lost her mind, because the blind, half-starved kitten was squirming in my grip so much I couldn't get him to swallow the life-saving milk I held out in a syringe. I was reasonably certain the kitten would die on my watch, and it would all be my fault. But my mother's confidence had calmed me, and the kitten, eventually named Midnight, survived.

It suddenly occurred to me as the wind picked up that I'd adopted Miles to prove my mother right; to put evidence to her conviction that I would be a good mother. Her comment had stuck with me over the years, past her death, through all my failed relationships, after I started trying to have children of my own. Her comment echoed back to me on sleepless nights and through fights with Nate. Even today I can still recall the exact tone of my mother's voice when she'd expressed her confidence in me, the slight tilt of her head. I stared out at the dispiriting horizon past the police station and thanked god she was no longer around to see what we'd become.

"You don't know what it's like to be Black!" Miles had yelled at me at the end of another of our long, drawn-out fights. And he was right, I didn't. But I'd told him that I didn't care, that he still needed to improve his attitude and get serious about school, that he was headed down a bad path. I'd spit the words at him, and at the memory of my fury, I now felt shame.

I took out my phone and tried my uncle's number another time. When there was still no answer I walked over to my car and got inside. I needed to lay down. I'd go back into the waiting area in a minute, but for now, I needed to rest in a place that was warm and familiar.

Evidence of Miles was everywhere in the car; his sunglasses on the dashboard, his favorite basketball on the passenger side floor, an old t-shirt and do-rag left on the seat. I glanced in the back and saw a flaming hot Doritos bag and a large blue Gatorade bottle. Squished into the armrest was the stem of a dandelion Miles had found a few weeks past and blown out the window like a child. The stem had been forgotten, left behind to grow old and withered.

I turned on the car for a little heat and the radio popped on louder than I'd expected. *Annie are you ok? Are you ok, Annie? Annie, are you ok?* I couldn't breathe. Michael Jackson was my son's favorite artist. It was as if he were speaking to me through the music. We'd played this very song, in fact, at Miles' first birthday party after we'd moved into our new neighborhood. I pushed the car seat back, closed my eyes, and recalled that time long ago.

Things had gone rather quickly, after deciding to move out of the neighborhood with the poor school and relentless bullies. Within a month I'd found a new apartment in a better (read: wealthier) part of town. Half the size of the apartment we'd had before, for double the rent. My commute to work was longer now too, but I told myself it was worth it. We settled in within weeks, bringing with us our wobbly dining room table, our colorful Marvel posters, and our few living plants.

I had been determined to do things right the second time, with the new school district and new neighborhood. I started by baking cookies the weekend after we moved in, putting them in plastic baggies tied with decorative bows and garnished with cards signed by both Miles and I. With my son by my side we walked door to door, handing the cookies out. I'd been told by a Black friend from our old neighborhood that it wouldn't be the worst idea in the world to introduce Miles to our new neighbors before anything bad happened, before someone saw him entering our apartment and called the police because he looked out of place. I made sure we stopped not just at all our neighbor's doors, but at nearby shops, and the local police station as well, handing out cookies and smiling brightly. I didn't tell Miles that we were making sure all his white neighbors knew he belonged in the neighborhood, that he lived here, that he was supposed to be seen walking the sidewalks. I told him merely that it was the neighborly thing to do, to introduce yourselves when you moved into a new home.

Luckily, it turned out to be a rather fun excursion. Together Miles and I discovered where the other boys Miles' age lived, and he made a couple of new friends. We also met the police chief who solidly shook Miles' hand and welcomed him to the neighborhood. And after hours of traipsing around the streets, we had a feel for the layout of the place, including the distance it took to get to the nearest playground with a swing set.

A few weeks later, I signed up as a parent volunteer in the school library, and took sick days at work to attend PTO meetings. I walked the halls of my son's new school, throwing out broad smiles to everyone I encountered, making my presence known as much as possible so the other teachers and staff would be aware that Miles had a mother who was involved and paying attention.

But in addition, I soon found that I had a secondary motive: I discovered that I was enjoying making new friends myself. I was now in a neighborhood where I, at least, fit in, and where the neighbors around me did and talked about things that were familiar. We watched the same Netflix shows, read the same books, could relate similar experiences from college and childhood. Our conversations flowed with an effortless I'd forgotten existed between strangers with a common upbringing. I sometimes missed the novelty of our old neighborhood, the unique foods and smells and unfamiliar languages, but more often than not, I simply felt at ease. While I didn't live in a big house like most of our new neighbors, I did share an unspoken tapestry of experience that made *my* adjustment into our new neighborhood, at least, easy.

It also, unfortunately, lulled me. The first time I was asked by a mother at Miles' school if I had any real children too, I was nonplussed. Miles was clearly confused as well. We glanced at each other with raised eyebrows while I simply repeated to the woman that Miles, here, was my son. Another mother, after volunteering with me for two hours during Miles' class Christmas party, asked me afterwards if I'd breastfed Miles when he was a baby. I looked at her, trying to fathom where the question was coming from, but she smiled back steadily, not batting an eye. I figured that she was either trying to subtly deduce the color of Miles' birth father, or, that she was doing one of those competitive mother things where you one-up the other mothers around you with how many good-parenting boxes you can check, including the difficulty of breastfeeding. I decided to assume the latter, and that this woman was trying so hard to portray acceptance of us, that she was willing to pretend not to see color at all. She was determined to treat us like she would any of the other families in the classroom, including by asking us the same questions she would anyone else, however inane they sounded. At least the majority of the people in our new neighborhood were *trying* to be accepting, even if they hadn't had much practice with it, and certainly weren't very good at it.

Miles made friends in his new school. One of the other mothers would text me and tell me her child was headed to the playground, and Miles would happily agree to join them. I was too nervous at first to let my son leave the apartment and walk to the playground by himself – he was getting older and more responsible and certainly knew *how* to get there by himself, as did the other boys, but I feared the image he portrayed, of a Black boy alone in a white neighborhood – so I continued to walk with him.

Miles joined the soccer team that first year, and then the basketball team, and then the flag football team, sports not offered at his previous school. I bought every team photo when they came out and proudly posted them on our refrigerator door, even though Miles stuck out in the pictures as the only brown kid in an all-white lineup, the single black kernel in an otherwise smooth cob of yellow-white corn.

I bought children's books on Martin Luther King Jr., Langston Hughes, Nat Turner, and W.E.B. DuBois, which Miles and I read together snuggled up in bed. I had heard how Barack Obama's mother had done the same thing with her son, waking Barack up at five in the morning before school even started, to make sure he got a regular dose of Black heritage. Miles put up with the extra readings, though he didn't always much like them.

The first Black figure Miles took a real interest in turned out to be Michael Jackson. I should have known the musician would be a strong draw for my son. A skinny talented personality who was Black, but also part white in some nebulous, hard-to-define manner. The first time Miles saw a video of Michael Jackson online, he watched it over and over and over again. Then he found another one and watched that one on a loop. Michael

Jackson had a posse of brothers, which Miles had always wished he could have, Michael Jackson was a great dancer, something Miles loved to do, and of course, Michael Jackson was from the relatively recent past, not from some dusty long-ago time that most of the historical figures I introduced him to were from, and that seemed to have no pertinent relevance to my then seven-year-old son.

For his birthday party that year Miles asked if we could have a Michael Jackson themed celebration. We were standing in an aisle at Party City, looking at the assortment of Thor, Spiderman, and Superman themed napkins, cups, and invitations, and I could tell that Miles was dissatisfied.

"What about the Hulk?" I asked, picking up a Hulk shaped invitation set. "You like the Hulk."

Miles shook his head.

"Spiderman?" I tried, pointing to the array of Spiderman paraphernalia. "Or," I strode over to the other side of the aisle, "Pokemon? I don't think anyone has had a Pokemon themed party yet this year."

Miles left me to walk up and down the long aisle, again.

"Ok," I said, when he returned to where I was standing. "We've been here half an hour already. You've got to choose." This was getting to be worse than the toy aisle at Target, which my son could get sucked into for entire afternoons if I let him.

"Where's the Michael Jackson stuff?" he turned to me and asked, as if it were inconceivable that there *wouldn't* be Michael Jackson themed party gear at Party City.

"Michael Jackson? Um, well, they probably don't have anything Michael Jackson themed, baby. He's from a few years ago," I tried to explain. "He's not as popular now."

Miles' face drooped and with it my heart.

"Let's go home," I said. "We can look for stuff online. Maybe there's Michael Jackson themed party stuff online."

But of course, there wasn't much online either. The best we were able to come up with was a Michael Jackson themed birthday cake, with the singer's image frosted on top from a photo

I could bring in, and a rhinestone covered glove and microphone ensemble from Amazon.

Miles was excited about the glove and microphone set, however. We'd have a singing contest at the birthday party, he told me, with each kid taking a turn with the glove and mic, singing and dancing to a Michael Jackson tune of their choosing. There would be candy prizes. And of course, the Michael Jackson frosted birthday cake at the end. Miles was happy with it, and I was happy that he was happy.

For days before the party Miles practiced singing various Michael Jackson songs in the mirror. I told him not to practice too much, it wouldn't be fair to the other kids, but he danced his way through every room in the apartment, singing all the Michael Jackson songs he had grown to know by heart.

On the day of the party, Miles' friends arrived eager, loud, and jumping up and down like they couldn't burn their candles down fast enough. When it came time for the singing contest, everyone sat in a semicircle and Miles explained how the mic worked and how everyone could pick whatever Michael Jackson song they wanted. Miles' friends all looked up at him like frogs on a log, blank, blinking expressions on their faces.

"Who's Michael Jackson?" one of them asked.

"Michael Jackson," Miles repeated, as if simply saying the singer's name again would bring awareness. But the blank expressions remained.

"I'm sure they know the tunes," I said hurriedly, "if not who sings them. Let's put them on." I pressed play on *Smooth Criminal* on my iPod, then *Thriller.* The boys smiled and squirmed to *Thriller*, but no one knew any of the words; there was no way anyone could sing or dance along to a karaoke type of Michael Jackson contest.

"How about the Jonas Brothers?" a boy named Hunter suggested, the rest of the boys nodding at the idea. No one but me noticed the disappointment drawn across my son's face at the suggestion.

* * *

Over the next couple of months Miles tried to individually bring some of his friends around to the magic of Michael Jackson. During playdates he'd tell them all about Michael Jackson's Neverland ranch, and the cool sunglasses and clothes the singer wore. But loving Michael Jackson was a solitary pursuit in our new neighborhood, and Miles eventually learned to keep the obsession to himself, bringing out his rhinestone glove and mic only when no one else was around. In front of his new friends, Miles learned to stick to singing Jonas Brothers lyrics with the rest of them. My son adjusted to his new neighborhood, while also coming to understand that he was somewhat apart from it. Over the years, almost without my realizing it, the apartness came to dominate the feeling of belonging.

# Chapter 11

***I*** sat up and turned the radio off. The music suddenly felt too loud, too intrusive. The car was warming up and I unzipped the top of my jacket. Thinking back, I guess I'd hoped we'd eventually just fit in. That given enough time we'd find our niche and snap into place – like those board puzzles Miles used to play with as a baby. The puzzle pieces always seemed oddly shaped and bulky at first, but with enough turning and pushing, they eventually found where they were supposed to go.

But instead, the feelings of alienation and apartness in our new neighborhood only seemed to grow. Outwardly it was a beautiful place – the streets were wide and well paved, there were medians with tall oaks and colorful tulips in the spring time, and the sidewalks were always clean and clear of debris. On any given Sunday morning I could look out our kitchen window while drinking coffee and see multiple well-dressed families, girls in patent leather shoes and pink skirts, fathers in crisp blue suits and swinging ties, walking down the neat sidewalks to the stone church on the corner.

When I'd first adopted Miles, religion hadn't been much on my mind. Nate and I had married in a civil ceremony and, except for the stomping of the glass at the end of our vows – a Jewish tradition Nate had always wanted to do for some reason, even though he wasn't in the least Jewish – our wedding had been devoid of religious significance. I hadn't considered a religious upbringing for Miles much beyond the lullabies I sang to him, until he got older and we moved to our new neighborhood and it became obvious every Sunday morning that we weren't walking to the church on the corner like so many of our neighbors.

"Where are all the people going?" Miles asked one day, joining me at the window.

"To church," I said, kissing the top of his head. "Do you want to go?"

But Miles shook his head, and I didn't really want to go myself, so I didn't push it.

We continued to watch the people outside together. I saw Jodi, the mom of a boy in Miles' third-grade class, and someone I thought I'd become friends with. We sat next to each other at PTO meetings, and once held a lemonade stand together on the corner with our two sons. We'd had a conversation about religion not that long ago, at the start of the fall season when red and orange leaves were newly littering the ground. I'd been bringing groceries in from my parked car when Jodi approached, her two-pound shih tzu leading the way.

"Rachel!" she called, waving with the hand that wasn't holding the leash.

I shifted a bag of groceries onto my hip and waved back.

We chatted for a few minutes about the weather, our leftover Halloween candy, and the upcoming Thanksgiving holiday. She told me how her son Hunter had already made up his Christmas wish list. I laughed, mentioning that Hanukkah was around the corner and that I needed to prepare for that holiday too.

"You're raising Miles Jewish?" Jodi asked, horror flitting briefly across her features. I felt the inner ramparts of my defenses rise; since Miles was born they'd become well-greased and smooth.

"Well, no," I replied, "I'm not really raising him anything, I'm just doing what we did when I was a kid. My mom was Jewish, actually, though my dad was Catholic, so we never did much of anything, or, sometimes, a bit of everything I guess." I laughed as if the grocery bag in my arms wasn't gaining in weight.

Jodi frowned and I felt some inexplicable need to make it go away.

"We did tend to celebrate more of the holidays with my dad's side of the family, Christmas and stuff, but Hanukkah was the one Jewish holiday we did because, well, come on, there are *eight* nights. *Eight* nights of presents." I laughed again, but Jodi still wasn't laughing with me.

"Was Miles' mother Jewish?"

"Miles' mother? I –"

"You know what I mean," Jodi interrupted. "It's just that, if she wasn't Jewish, if she was a Christian, then you have to raise Miles as a Christian too."

I nearly lost the grip on my groceries. I stood for a minute readjusting while the shih tzu pulled on his leash. Jodi and I stood there in silence until the only thing I could think to do was pick up another bag, turn, and head into the apartment building.

Later, I tried to wrap my head around what Jodi had said, but it was so illogical, in so many ways, I didn't know where to start. Religion wasn't genetic, like heart disease. Besides, *I* was Miles's mother. Did Jodi not understand that? Did Jodi think *I* didn't understand that? Was I really supposed to raise my son Christian while I was nothing of the sort? How was that supposed to work?

But what really bothered me, at heart, was that her question was proof she didn't see Miles and I in a traditional mother-son relationship at all. I had always seen adoption as something that happened, kind of like birth, that once it was done, there was no going back. You moved forward as a united family, like any other natural-born family, into the future together. I knew with certainty that I was Miles's mother, that he was my son, and that I would raise him and love him and teach him and reprimand him as if he were my very own flesh and blood. If it seemed inconceivable that I would raise a child of my womb in a religion I myself did not follow, then it should seem inconceivable that I would raise Miles that way. But it was becoming apparent to me more and more every day, that other people did not see us that way. Other people, even apparent friends, seemed unable to leap the barrier that was forever forefront in their minds, that I was not, and would never be, Miles's *actual* mother. The realization made me angry, but it also hurt my heart.

* * *

The following Sunday after breakfast I sat with Miles on the couch and handed him a small book with gilt lettering on the cover.

"What's this?" he asked, turning the book over curiously in his hands.

"A bible. Sharelle left it with you in the hospital."

Miles' eyes opened wide and he leafed through the thin pages. "Is this her handwriting?" he asked.

I looked over his shoulder at the inside back cover where the date of Miles' birth was written in a shaky black ink. "I imagine so."

There was silence for a long moment and then Miles asked, "Do you think I was meant to be your son?"

I shook my head, as if I didn't understand.

"I mean, do you think God meant for us to be together? Do you think I was destined to be your son?"

I knew the answer my son wanted to hear. He wanted to hear that God had chosen for us to be together as a family, that it was inevitable, that it was ordained by a higher power and irrefutably meant to be. He wanted there to be a reason that the woman who'd written his birth date in a thin black scrawl on the inside cover of a small blue book hadn't had to give him up for no good reason. Miles definitely didn't want to hear that we'd waited for years to have a baby, any baby, that by the end Nate and I would have taken anything that was breathing.

"Of course," I said. "It couldn't have been any other way."

Miles nodded and closed the bible and handed it back to me.

"You don't want to look through it some more?"

"No. Just keep it for me, ok?"

"Of course," I said, promising to keep it safe. "Do you want to go to church sometime?" I asked. "The one on the corner, where Hunter and Josh and everyone else goes?"

Miles paused, and then asked, "Is that where my birth mom went?"

"Well, no, I don't know where she went. If she went."

"No," Miles said with certainty. "We wouldn't fit in there."

"No," I agreed, "we probably wouldn't."

# Chapter 12

***I*** pressed dial on my uncle's number yet again, and stared out the car window while it rang. If I was calling the wrong number I would have gotten a recording, or someone unfamiliar on the line. But it didn't go to a recorded operator or a stranger, instead it rang and rang into an expanding, endless, suffocating void. I imagined my uncle at the other end of the line, looking down at his vibrating phone, recognizing my number, and then shrugging as he walked away from it. I understood that Uncle Ian was most likely just asleep, or indisposed, not willfully ignoring my call, but it was easy to imagine him ignoring me in order to teach me a lesson. Whatever was happening, I was determined to keep calling until he answered.

I got out of the car and left its warmth to head back into the station. I didn't want the police to think I'd disappeared and that my son had been abandoned. I wasn't going anywhere, and they were going to let me see him, even if I had to make a scene to make that happen.

But when I stepped passed the threshold back into the police station, I found a scene already in progress. The woman I'd been sitting across from was now standing in the middle of the waiting area, arguing with an officer that was in front of her, one hand on his holster, the other pointing in her face. "Lower your phone," he commanded loudly. "Now." I glanced at a sign high on the wall with a picture of a crossed-out video recorder. "No video recordings in the station." The officer lunged forward but the woman swerved before he was able to grab the phone I now saw in her hand.

"I done, I done," she said, dropping the device into her oversized purse. She turned sharply from the officer and walked back to her seat. Everyone stared at her.

It occurred to me only in that moment that the room was being monitored. That within seconds, an officer could be through the side door, hand on hip, authority bearing down on you. All of my intentions to enter the station and demand action for my son disappeared. I was out of my element. I'd been at the station for over an hour, and I still had no idea how the place worked. I realized that I could make things worse for Miles if I wasn't careful. It had taken me decades to learn, but I was old enough now to know that I shouldn't make things worse by blindly arguing with those in charge.

I returned to my seat, across from the woman who was now busy rifling through her purse. She glanced my way and gave me a wry, half-smile. I returned it, grateful for any small bit of sympathetic commiseration. Eventually she brought out a compact and powdered her nose, pressing her lips together in a frown. Carefully she patted the mound of hair behind her wrap. I recognized what she was doing. She was restoring her confidence through a reassurance of her good looks.

My son sometimes did that too. I know that all mother's think their children are the handsomest, the best looking in their class, but in Miles' case it really was true. Miles had been blessed with large, almond-shaped eyes, a strong jaw, and dimples that made your heart melt. When we finally got a handle on his hair, he was breathtaking. It had taken awhile to get a handle on his hair, however. I only realized how bad I was doing when Miles came home from school in the fourth grade and told me that the other kids teased him about it, calling it pokey.

"Pokey?" I asked.

"Yeah, they say it pokes their fingers when they touch it."

"Why are they touching it?"

"I don't know," Miles said, shrugging, "but they do."

When Miles was very young, I had dealt with his hair by cutting it myself; by grabbing a peanut clipper and shaving his head close every three to four weeks. In my experience, most mothers cut their children's hair when they were young, and even if it looked somewhat unprofessional, no one cared. Having your mother give you a bad haircut was a rite of passage. One white mother we had a playdate with when Miles was very young didn't even seem to realize I was the one taking care of Miles's hair. Apropos of nothing she turned to me during the playdate and said, "It must be nice to have a child whose hair doesn't grow." After I got over my surprise at her ignorance, I felt a tug of pride that she thought my son's hair looked just like every other Black boy's hair.

But as Miles got older, and in particular after we moved into the all-white neighborhood, he began to struggle against the close-cropped shaves. I sat him down for the usual haircut one day and he turned to me before we started and asked if he could have Henry Danger hair - that blonde kid on Nickelodeon who pretends to be a superhero, and has smooth, flowing yellow locks.

"O-kaay," I'd replied in the moment, buying time to think of a good way to explain to my son that he couldn't have the blonde, straight hair he wanted. I eventually told him that none of us actually ever got the hair we wanted. I had always wanted bouncy red curls, like Annie, when I was his age, and I never got them. No one in life got exactly what they wanted. He nodded, and for the moment, seemed to understand.

A few weeks later, however, when it was time for another buzz cut, Miles asked for Harry Potter hair. This time, I visibly sighed. "Honey," I told him straight, "you've got dark, curly, Black boy hair. You will always have this kind of hair, like, like," I struggled for a minute to think of a character he could identify with, "like George in Captain Underpants."

Miles nodded, he was listening, though I wasn't certain if he was understanding.

"It doesn't matter how I cut your hair, baby, or what we try to do to it," I said, feeling vaguely as if this were my fault, "but we can't straighten your hair like Harry Potter, or Henry

Danger, or most of the other superheroes. I'm sorry baby. But," I added, touching my son's cheek, "I think your hair is beautiful. I don't think you should want to change a thing about it."

Miles nodded and didn't argue, but after a minute he asked if we could at least grow it longer. "Sure," I said, "of course." We put the clippers away and didn't bring them out again for months. His hair grew longer, the curls tighter, the look a bit unruly. I didn't concern myself with it much until Miles told me the other kids were calling it pokey.

"Let's go to a stylist," I said to Miles that day. "Get your hair done right, by somebody who knows what they're doing."

"Can't you just do it? Can't you make it look better?" Miles seemed to think I could do anything, which was sweet, but not always helpful.

"I can't. I don't know how. I never went to school to study hair," I said, trying to explain things. "There are people who practice and train to style hair really well. It's their job, like mommy's job is at the bank. We can take you to someone whose job is hair."

"Ok," Miles agreed, and I suddenly felt terrible I'd waited so long to take him.

Part of the reason, to be honest, that I'd waited so long was that there was nowhere in our neighborhood I could take him. I called a few local shops to make an appointment, but they all told me they didn't cut African American hair. I couldn't ask any of my white neighbors where they went, of course. I thought about it and recalled a barber shop I'd driven by in our old neighborhood, a cute place with an actual barber pole out front and an entirely Black clientele - as best could be seen through the window - inside. I figured we'd try there.

We drove up one cool spring afternoon and parked in a small back lot with crumbling asphalt, the difference between our old and new neighborhoods apparent. Cigarette butts littered the ground, loud music emanated from broken windows across the street, and cars raced by us so fast Miles stumbled. We approached the barber shop door together, Miles' hand in mine, our feet stepping past the entrance one after the other. As the door tinkled shut behind us, a wide sea of black male faces confronted us. I had expected to be the only white person in the establishment, that wasn't a surprise, but what I hadn't prepared for, was to be the only woman in the room. There wasn't a single other female in sight. My ignorant mother mistake for that day, had been to fail to realize that barber shops in the Black community were mainly for men. Women had their own salons. And obviously, white people didn't come around to either.

An embarrassed heat came over me in waves, but I walked forwards, pretending that nothing was amiss, feeling like I couldn't back out now. All conversation died around us, as if when we moved forward, we parted a Red Sea of sound. I tried to smile and look everyone in the eye. I pretended to know what I was doing.

After what appeared to be the salon owner acknowledged our existence with a head nod, Miles and I sat on a corner bench and waited. A thin, elderly man with warm brown folds of skin eventually came over to us. "Where you from?" he asked.

I urged Miles to answer the man. "Here," my son said coolly.

"My name's Aaron," the man said, holding out his hand for Miles to shake. Miles reached over and took it. I could tell, despite the hesitancy of his manner, that Miles liked Aaron, he liked being spoken to as if he were an adult. The two of them struck up a conversation, and I switched seats with my son to get out of their way.

As they talked, I glanced around the barbershop. It was L shaped, with the entrance door at the corner of the L where the two sides came together. A couple of barber chairs and a very long mirror were along the length of the long side, and a black bench snug against the wall was placed along the short side. A number of other customers besides ourselves were waiting for haircuts. Three large televisions hung from the ceiling in various spots, and while no one seemed to be watching them, at odd intervals a customer would shout out some commentary, and everyone would immediately respond with grunts of agreement or disagreement. The room would go from near silence to a chorus of interjections and shouts, to near silence again as the televisions themselves were barely audible. There seemed to be an invisible communication mechanism swirling around the establishment, one which I was definitely not privy to. I felt stupid. I wondered if there was somewhere else I could have taken Miles for a haircut. I cursed the world for being so segregated.

Then I glanced at my son, and his new friend Aaron, and saw how happily they were chatting away. My son had turned his whole body towards Aaron and was actively engaged in the conversation. Aaron noticed me watching them and smiled. I relaxed. Miles was still too young to notice all of my dumb mistakes, and how little I understood what I was doing as his mother. But, I also knew, he was growing up, and one day he would notice everything I did, and be embarrassed by me. One day, but not yet that day.

When it was at last my son's turn to get his hair cut, Aaron pushed him forwards towards a chair and he plopped himself down as if he'd sat there a hundred times. Gone was the fidgetiness my son exhibited every time I cut his hair, no more were the constant interruptions and questions about everything that popped into his head. Miles sat in the barber's chair a paragon of deference and respectability, and I wondered for a second whose child he was.

When we left the barbershop a little while later Miles had a smile on his face, a fancy new haircut that was definitely not pokey, and a new set of Black friends that I knew we would be returning to. I should have taken him to get a proper haircut years earlier, but in the moment, I focused my annoyance not on myself, but on our neighborhood, and on the fact that there was nowhere closer like this for us to go. It had taken nearly the whole of a Saturday afternoon to drive out to the old neighborhood and wait for a haircut; I now didn't have time to go grocery shopping like I'd wanted to. But looking at my smiling son in the rear-view mirror, I knew it had been worth it.

When Miles returned to school the following Monday, things seemed to improve. He told me the other kids liked his haircut, Hunter even telling him that he looked just like Fresh Prince and yelling a friendly, "Hey, homey!" to him in the hall.

"He says what?" I asked.

"'Hey, homey,'" Miles repeated, proud, but now a little uncertain. "It's like I'm one of them," he paused, "right?"

# Chapter 13

***'H**omey,'* I learned, was everyone's favorite way to reference Miles at school, but 'brotha' and 'bro' were in use as well. Miles started coming home repeating the nicknames in a ridiculous Black patois, which I hated, but tried not to show. He started listening to hip-hop and funk and asking me to change the radio station in the car if the Jonas Brothers or Taylor Swift came on. One day, Miles switched his school email avatar from a nondescript letter "M" to an up-close selfie of his growling, grimacing face. He looked the image of a stereotypical thug.

I hoped that our uniqueness in the neighborhood was appreciated. I wanted to believe that Miles' growing embrace of his Blackness was valued even by the other parents. Didn't rich white people talk about the importance of diversity all the time? Didn't they say they wanted their children to have a wide array of friends, with a wide array of perspectives? I sometimes suspected this was a talking point more than a truth, but I pushed such doubts aside. If diversity and integration were true values, actual effort would be made to include us, even as our differences increasingly stood out. More often than not, however, the opposite happened.

By fifth grade I learned that there were events around the neighborhood that we were often left out of. There was a run for charity that a mother in the neighborhood organized, but somehow, we never got the email. There was a youth book club that formed, where boys from Miles class would get together and read and act out the Dog Man books, but we were only told about them after they ended. I did learn at a PTO meeting that there were finishing classes in the neighborhood, evening get-togethers with white gloves and formal suits where small boys waltzed with equally small girls dolled up in gowns and tiaras. I laughed out loud when I'd heard this, but it was true, and also, the registration deadline had passed.

Some of it, I suspected, was that we were just late to the neighborhood. Young mothers bonded over their young children in kindergarten, and if you moved into a district even just a few years into elementary school, you were irredeemably late to the party. Phone numbers had already been exchanged. Important friendships had already gelled. But I couldn't help thinking that our treatment was more than that. It seemed as if we were regularly rebuffed at events and from places around town.

When Miles turned ten I noticed that a few of his teeth had turned inward and that he needed braces to correct them. I called the local orthodontist that all the mothers in the neighborhood recommended. Jodi had assured me, in fact, that this was a great practice with a doctor that had already treated two of her older children. On the morning of Miles' appointment I took a half day off work, and we first went to a pancake restaurant for breakfast. I wanted Miles to enjoy a few more carefree meals before his mouth turned, for a number of months, into a hardwired battleground.

It was a chilly, overcast morning when we left the house, and either because of the weather or because it was the middle of the week, the restaurant had few customers that day. We ordered eggs and pancakes and played our old game of *Which Do You Prefer*.

"Basketball or football?" I asked.

"Basketball," Miles said without hesitation. "Cars or boats?" he asked me.

"Cars," I replied. "Cupcakes or ice cream?" I asked, forcing my son to choose between his two favorite desserts. It was an impossible choice and Miles frowned for a moment. "I can't choose!" he finally yelled, and we both devolved into laughter.

We were still smiling when we arrived at the orthodontist's office half an hour later, but the receptionist behind the desk lost her smile when we walked in. She glanced first at me, then at Miles, then at me again. With a pinched face she told us to wait, abruptly closing the sliding glass partition between us. I didn't know if we should sit down, or continue to stand where we were. My son ambled over to the seating area, nodding to a friend from his class, and turned on his tablet. A number of minutes later the glass partition slid back open and the aggrieved receptionist asked if I'd brought my papers with me.

"Yes," I replied confidently. I was always well organized. My husband had always been mystified at how I could find ten-year old dishwasher warranties, or notes from important events made years before. With a smile I handed over Miles', and my own for good measure, insurance cards to the receptionist.

"Not these," she said, pushing them away as if they carried disease. "Your guardian papers."

"My what?"

"Your guar-di-an papers," she repeated, as if I were dumb.

"No," I shook my head. "This is the orthodontist's office, right?" I looked around at the dental decorations on the wall, the plastic over-sized molar on the desk holding a set of identical white pens. "We have an appointment. At eleven. With Dr. Nagler."

The woman didn't respond.

"For an evaluation," I added, this time as if she were dumb.

"Yes, well, we can't see the boy unless you can provide papers from his mother, or other guardian of the state, that says we can treat him."

My mouth opened, and then shut. "I'm sorry," I finally said, "but I don't know what you're asking. That is my son," I said, pointing to Miles. He looked up, and waved. "I am his mother. We are here for his first appointment." My voice edged higher and I saw, out of the corner of my eye, that the other patients in the waiting area were starting to watch the scene unfold, including Miles' friend Josh.

"If you are his mother," the woman replied with skepticism, "then I need to see some adoption papers."

"Excuse me?" I asked in disbelief. I narrowed my eyes and tried to stare down my nose at this ignorant receptionist, to indicate to her that I was offended by her suggestion, but she failed to acknowledge my nonverbal accusation and remained quiet, still.

"Unless you can prove you are his mother, we can't see the boy," she finally said.

Five minutes later we were back in the car, my son asking me why we were leaving so soon. "Isn't the doctor going to see me?" he asked. "Do I still get a lollipop?"

"Not today."

I started backing out of the parking lot. "Why?" Miles asked.

I stopped driving and put the car in park. I turned towards my son and racked my brain for a suitable answer to his valid question. One that was honest, but that at the same time wouldn't make him feel bad for being him. How did one explain racism to a child? Was he old enough to understand? Did I go back and explain America's institutional history to him? Or did I just tell him that there were stupid people in this world, and sometimes we ran into them, and when we did, we just had to leave?

"Was it because I'm Black?" Miles's voice interrupted my thoughts.

I looked directly at my son in the back seat of the car.

"No," I said. "It was because I'm white."

Miles nodded, looked out the window, and I told him we could go get a bag of lollipops from the drug store.

* * *

A week later I called the orthodontist's office and asked if they queried every new patient for adoption papers, or just the ones that looked like ours. The condescending receptionist claimed that they asked every single new patient for papers to make sure they could legally treat them. As if it were some sort of a common scam for people around St. Louis to steal little Black children and take them to the orthodontist for expensive dental care.

"Bullshit," I said, and hung up on her.

But then I was left with the ordeal of having to find a new orthodontist, one which the neighborhood mothers obviously didn't know to recommend, one that saw little Black boys with little white mothers and didn't have a problem with it.

I loved my son so much. I saw our bond as so obvious, so incontrovertible, so inevitable, that when it was questioned, I was stunned. It took my breath away, every time, like a punch to the gut, and I often needed more than a minute to recover before I could appropriately respond. But what was the appropriate response? At nights, after putting Miles to bed and kissing his forehead and gazing at the perfection of his round, dimpled cheeks, I'd go to the kitchen and make myself a cup of tea, and stew over the day's events and how I should have responded to them. I'd imagine the perfect quip, not too funny, not too light-hearted, just insulting enough to make the ignorant receptionist or cashier or bank teller realize the obnoxiousness of their own behavior. I'd imagine them begging forgiveness, the light of understanding at last dawning in their eyes. I'd imagine my gracious reply then, calm, kind, conciliatory, with just a touch of haughtiness thrown in for good measure.

By the second cup of tea I'd be imagining what it would be like if, instead, whatever insult Miles and I had endured that day just hadn't happened at all. What would it be like if we could sail into the doctor's office, or the bank branch, or the YMCA, and no one, absolutely no single person, assumed anything was wrong, or odd, or even just noteworthy about us? If instead of consternation and side-eye, we got kindness and affection, candies for Miles and winks of maternal understanding for me. Pats on the back and garrulous queries about if Miles was going to grow up to be a doctor or lawyer, instead of a basketball player or football player, which seemed to be the *only* two occupations *anyone* ever considered for my Black son.

I yearned to smoke a cigarette at such times. Open the back door of my kitchen, stretch my legs into the cool evening air, and stare into the dark sky as I inhaled, and then slowly exhaled, the poisonous tar that had killed my own mother. But that wasn't what responsible mothers did. Responsible mothers took care of themselves, so they could take care of their children. Miles had no one left any longer but me. His birth mother was gone. We never found out who his birth father was. Nate had disappeared, fled to a different house and a different life with a different soon-to-be wife. Miles had no siblings, he had no living or involved grandparents. If I were no longer around to take care of him, who would?

Sometimes my mind pursued an answer to that question, and what it imagined frightened me. I would see myself dying from cancer in my forties like my mother, and as Miles was taken out of my feeble embrace, he was handed over to another mother waiting in the wings, a better mother, one that looked more like him. They had the same roundness of cheek, the same almond-curved eyes, the same caramel brown skin. Miles was taken from my embrace as I lay in the hospital bed and, instead of crying at the loss, he was overcome with joy at the discovery of his new, more appropriate mother. The mother that matched his every need, and that no one ever questioned he belonged with.

# Chapter 14

*T*he middle-aged man sitting by the end-table with the coffee stains suddenly stood up, glanced around the station, and strode out the door. He'd been so quiet for so long I'd nearly forgotten his presence. I sat for a moment wondering what could have been so important that he'd waited in a police station for over an hour on a Saturday night, but then so unimportant that he could just get up and leave. I glanced at my watch. It was now 4:26 a.m. Perhaps he'd decided to go get his own cup of coffee and he'd be back. But his departure was so abrupt, and his stride so determined, it felt like he wouldn't be returning. My eyes connected with the woman across from me and we both shrugged.

I looked across the room at the police officer behind the partition. Another one down, his expression seemed to imply. Just two more to go. The woman across from me pulled a pair of earbuds from her purse and settled in to listen to some music. She wasn't going anywhere, she seemed to be saying, to anyone who was looking. I heard the faint, but unmistakable, strains of Lauryn Hill's *Nothing Even Matters*. In the relative quiet of the station I picked up more of her playlist, Black Sheep, Drake, Sa-Roc. It was comforting. It drew me back to the homeless shelter Miles and I used to volunteer at when he was in middle school; similar songs would play in the kitchen there while I washed dishes and Miles played with the other children his age in the main room.

It wasn't long after Miles started sixth grade that we started volunteering. He'd been coming home from his first year of middle school complaining about all of the things he didn't have that the other kids did: game boxes, sports jerseys, expensive shoes. At first I tried sitting Miles down and explaining to him what a budget was and what we could and couldn't afford. I wanted him to understand where I was coming from when I said no. I also wanted to turn his perspective around by expressing the belief that being different was not bad, that it meant you were unique and special. Experiences were opportunities, I told him, and having to work to earn things meant that they were more valued.

I couldn't convince Miles, however. He listened to me, and nodded, but he just wanted to fit in. If his classmates played 2K, he wanted to play 2K. If his friends were wearing Nike Airs, he wanted Nike Airs. A quadcopter drone with remote control? A blue and black one please.

By middle school the big fashion trend amongst the boys in the neighborhood were the named sports jerseys, whether it was Brady, Mahomes, Messi, Maroon, or Antetokounmpo, the kids in the neighborhood had them all and Miles wanted some too. The problem was that we couldn't afford genuine NFL, NBA, or FIFA jerseys. I tried buying knock-offs from an online store in China, but the kids could tell the fakes right away. Disappointed, Miles would ask for other things, like the motorized scooter Josh had, or the PlayStation Carson had. I explained to Miles a number of times that we couldn't afford such things, but he seemed constitutionally unable to digest the meaning of a limited budget, and just asked for the coveted items again weeks later.

I hated saying no to Miles. I wanted him to feel that he belonged in the neighborhood, but it was hard when Miles constantly compared himself to the wealthier kids around us and always found us wanting. Our home couldn't compete, and every playdate or birthday party was a bargain with the devil where I was glad of the social interaction and the friends I thought he was making, but where I also knew Miles would return to our apartment begging for whatever item we didn't have, I couldn't afford, and he didn't need.

"Hunter has an Xbox," Miles told me one day as I picked him up from school. I was starting to hate hearing that kid's name.

"And you have a Switch," I replied.

"Yes. But I want an Xbox."

"What do you need two gaming consoles for?" I asked, unlocking the car doors. "You can only play one at a time."

Miles rolled his eyes, and the sun glinted off the car roof as we got inside. "The Xbox and the Switch have different games. Plus, the new Xbox comes with a Fortnite Ultimate Pass, so it's totally worth it. You get a new skin every month, and…"

I looked around the car. Did I leave my purse at work again? I was so pathologically forgetful it was ridiculous. Nate used to say that I was really very smart, but not very bright at all. That had always been funny, until it got repetitive.

"…so you agree," Miles concluded, as I gave up and started the car and we pulled into traffic.

"Agree to what?"

"Were you listening to me at all? A new Xbox."

"A new Xbox?"

"Yes. It makes sense. Here's why…"

I tried listening to my son, but I was too tired. And I was embarrassed to admit I'd blanked on everything he'd said a minute before.

"Ok," I said.

"Ok?" Miles was too eager for more words.

I nodded, knowing full well it was a bad idea.

He's a good kid, I reasoned to myself two weeks later when the credit card bill arrived and I realized I couldn't pay it. I didn't want to take the Xbox back, but I stared at my bill and finally had to admit that something had to change. I needed to make Miles more aware of budgetary limits. I needed to make him realize that it was ok not to have things, that there were people, most people in fact, who didn't have multiple gaming consoles.

I picked my son up from school the following Friday and instead of driving straight home, we went to McDonalds. Miles loved McDonalds, though he was aging out of the happy meals and had begun supersizing regular orders and actually finishing all of the fries that came with it.

We sat down in a sticky orange booth and Miles pulled the tray of food towards him. He began stuffing handfuls of fries into his mouth between extra-large bites of hamburger. There was something so satisfying, as a mother, about watching your child consume a large meal.

I took a bite of my own hamburger and told Miles we were going to do something different that evening.

"Mmmm?"

"We're going to volunteer. At a shelter."

Miles swallowed his food. "A shelter?"

"It's a place where people go if they need somewhere to sleep for the night. So they don't have to sleep outside," I added.

Miles tilted his head to the side. "Outside? Where would you sleep outside?"

My son was very pragmatic and always wanted practical answers to things. "On a park bench. Or, or on the sidewalk, like that homeless person we came across downtown once, do you remember that?"

Miles thought about it, but couldn't recall the incident.

"That's ok, it was years ago, when you were younger."

Miles took a sip of his drink. "Why would anyone sleep outside though?"

"If you don't have a home. If you've lost your home, say."

I could tell that Miles was now wondering how a person lost their home.

"The point is, there are people less fortunate than us. There are people that could use a little help. Heck, *everyone* can use a little help in their life at some point. But tonight, we're going to go help other people out for a bit."

Miles nodded and finished the last of his hamburger.

A few minutes later we were driving to a homeless shelter in downtown St. Louis. It was a family shelter, for mothers (primarily) and their young kids, and as I'd hoped, there were children there about Miles' own age. He was hesitant at first, taking tentative steps into the building and not touching anything. For a minute I was afraid my son would act the snob, and complain about the dinginess of the place, but my fears were allayed when a kid around his own age came up to Miles and invited him to play. Together they explored the tub of donated toys. A few minutes later they were racing cars and setting up battlefields of brown and green plastic soldiers.

I went to the kitchen and washed dishes for about an hour, and when I returned to the main room my son was still playing. I sat at a table between a pair of mothers that were also watching the children and their games.

"Which one's yours?" I asked the woman on my right. She pointed to a boy in a Ninja Turtles shirt, but said nothing. The woman on my left pointed out her children, and then we were all quiet. We watched the boys play, and for the first time in a long time, if I looked away, when I returned my gaze to the group of children it took me a minute to discern which one was my own son. I was so used to his being the only Black child in a crowd, and it being so easy to just glance over and spot him when I needed to, that I had to smile now that it took me a second to find him.

I became aware that the lady on my left was watching me out of the corner of her eye. "Did you bring that boy?" she asked.

I nodded, unable to keep the pride from my voice, "Yes, that's my son."

"Hmphf," she grunted, and I felt uneasy.

The words of that long-ago article came back to me, telling me that I had no right to adopt a Black child, telling me that I would be a bad mother to an African American boy, telling me that I had no idea how to raise a young Black man right. I looked down at the table top and realized only then that I'd been expecting some sort confirmation from the other women around the table, or dare I say, even praise. I always got it so easily from the crowds of white mothers, the sympathetic head nod, or the *sotto voce* whisper about what a great thing I'd done, adopting an *unwanted child.* But in the shelter all I got was suspicion. I realized they were probably thinking that I was one of those idealistic, naïve, annoying white women who presume to think they're saving the world. I worried they were shaking their heads in sorrow for my son, who was going to grow up soft and unprepared for the realities of this world.

I wanted to say something. I desperately searched for the right phrase or anecdote that would prove I was ok; that *I,* at least, if not all those other white mothers, knew what I was doing. But of course, there was no perfect phrase or anecdote. Of course, I didn't have any idea what I was doing. And so I sat there, and none of us said a thing.

Eventually, a more talkative mother joined the table and got something of a conversation going. She was kind and inclusive, asking all of us questions about our children. I appreciated her bringing me into the conversation, but when I got up to go to the bathroom, I couldn't help but assume that she tore into me along with the rest of the mothers.

I decided not to let my unease stop us from returning to the shelter. Every three weeks, on a Friday after school, I'd pick Miles up, listen to him complain about math or spelling while he simultaneously inhaled hamburgers and french fries, and then together we headed over to the shelter for the rest of the evening. I think Miles even started looking forward to the visits, the shelter a place where he inevitably found a posse of playmates for any new game he could invent. He found the group of brothers he'd always wanted, like Michael Jackson had.

About three months into our volunteering, on the drive home to our apartment in the dusk of an early evening, Miles asked an uncomfortable question. Miles had a habit of asking important, embarrassing, or otherwise significant questions while we were driving in the car. I don't know what it was about sitting in the backseat of a moving vehicle and gazing out the window that inspired him, but I'd look up through my rear-view mirror while singing along to *Man in the Mirror* and he'd suddenly glance at me and ask, "How are babies made?" or "How'd your mom die?" or "Is daddy ever coming back?"

The first time he did this I'd searched for a convenient place to pull over and stop the car, so I could turn around and look him in the eye while I explained how a man brought the seed, and a woman brought the egg, and together they made a baby. But I soon found that Miles preferred it if I kept driving. He liked the *inability* of my being able to face him while I answered these tough questions.

"Why is everyone there Black?" he asked me that day as the streetlights flicked repetitively through the windshield. The question hit like a punch to the gut and I suddenly felt very, very sad, both because he'd asked a perfectly good question with no good answer, but also because I hadn't even thought to address the issue before we started volunteering. Of course he was going to notice the huge color disparity of the shelter, as opposed to his school. Of course he was going to wonder why things were that way. But where did I begin trying to explain it? How does one make institutional racism explicable to an eleven-year-old child?

I tried to make eye contact with Miles through the rear-view mirror, but his head was turned, and he was gazing out the window while he waited for my answer. I wished I could see what the world had in store for him. I wished I could prepare him for where he'd end up in twenty years, in a hospital as a respected doctor tending to patients, or, in a hospital on a gurney bleeding from a gunshot wound. Either way, would he understand what was happening, and why? Or would he be filled with an accumulated, unexpressed, irrepressible anger and confusion over the vagaries of life? Whatever happened, would I be able to help him with it?

I opened my mouth and gave Miles a long, rambling answer to his important question that included a history of slavery and a primer on the basics of American capitalism. I reminded him that life was unfair, and that some people were born with more opportunity than others. I talked to him for the whole car ride home, and when we entered our apartment, I told him he could ask me any questions he wanted. He looked at me then, paused, and asked if he could forego his homework and play Fortnite for the rest of the evening. I sighed, nodded, and let him go.

The hardest thing about being a parent, I thought then as I'd thought many times before, wasn't the expense of having a child, or the time involved in raising a child, or the arguments, discipline, and hours of incomprehensible math homework, it was the worrying and doing your best but having absolutely no idea if what you were doing was good enough. It was being responsible for the tough decisions, but never knowing if you made the right calls. There was no answer key you could flip through, that told you that yes, moving had been the right change to make. Or no, volunteering at the shelter wasn't really a good idea. There was no way to ever really know if you were doing things right.

# Chapter 15

***"H**ullo?"* My uncle answered the phone and in my surprise I nearly dropped it. I rushed outside the station to talk with a bit of privacy. "Hello?" My uncle's familiar, raspy voice came through again, louder this time. The cool night air whipped my hair and jacket.

"Uncle Ian, it's me, Rachel." I watched as a couple of cars drove by on the highway overpass in the distance. "It's been a long time," I said. "I'm sorry I'm calling so late. How are you?" In the silence that followed I watched a few more cars drive past.

"What do you want?" my uncle finally replied. "No, wait, let me guess." And without possibility of interruption he dove into an extended harangue on why I must be calling him. It was as if the years of silence between us had been but a moment, and we were continuing our last argument exactly where we'd left off. "And because of those bad decisions," my uncle surmised, "you need money."

I recalled my mother telling me how her older brother had once defended her from a bully when they were children. She was being dragged by the hair by an older boy at school and my uncle, though shorter and decidedly smaller at the time, had started a fight to free her. Uncle Ian had been roughed up a bit himself but the bully had been embarrassed in front of his friends, which was worse, and so he'd left my mother alone after that. Every time Uncle Ian said or did something stupid or mean, my mother would remind me of what he'd done for her that one time as a child. It didn't matter that over the subsequent years he'd beaten her up himself, or stolen her allowance, or pulled apart her favorite dolls until the stuffing covered the floor like the fluffy innards of a heaven-sent horror show. Everyone had some good in them, my mother would tell me, you just had to wait for the moment when it came out.

But I'd yet to have such a moment with Uncle Ian myself. The majority of our interactions since Miles had been born involved snide or condescending comments to me or my son, hurtful judgements about our lifestyle that he didn't deserve to make. I wondered for years why I was supposed to put up with it; why Uncle Ian get to be an ass, just because he was my uncle.

"Well, no--," I tried to say, but he wasn't done yet.

"And let me tell you where I've been…" I gripped my jacket around me as the wind continued to cut. A solitary leaf from a tree that was nowhere in sight skittered past my feet.

Relationships were hard. Life was hard. And I'd never been very good at maintaining interpersonal connections, as evidenced by the solitary life that Miles and I now led. I wasn't proud of it; I would have preferred to have close family and even closer friends, but over the years I'd often felt that I'd had to choose between friendships, or forthrightness; trust, or the truth. And in the end, I couldn't help but give in to honesty, and I'd opened my mouth and pointed out to cousins and aunts and uncles and neighbors the way their actions were hurtful, and how their offhanded comments could be perceived. No one ever appreciated my insights.

So people dropped out of our lives, and I never did do much to stem the tide. I was pretty sure that a better person than me would have been able to navigate such minefields without making everyone upset, but I seemed wholly unable to do it. It hurt too much. It cut too close. I stopped seeing Uncle Ian after the divorce when he'd taken Nate's side, but to be honest, the worst thing he'd ever done had been a few years after that when he'd made me - for the first and only time - question if adopting Miles had been worth it.

Miles had been about to turn twelve, and the other mothers in the neighborhood were talking about sending their kids to an overnight camp for one, or even two-week sessions. At first, the idea struck me as ludicrous, giving your child away for multiple weeks at a time, trusting complete strangers to take care of, love, and be there if, and when, he needed them. And Miles would definitely need them, he was only eleven years old. He still had a favorite blanket and wasn't certain there *weren't* monsters in his closet at night.

Yet, I wanted my son to fit in around the neighborhood and do what all the other kids were doing, and I did like the idea that sleeping in the woods would teach my son resilience and independence. In the end, I'd scrounged together the money for the expensive overnight camp, bought the over-sized duffel bag and heavy-duty flashlights required, and sent Miles away for two weeks in the middle of June, just before his twelfth birthday.

It took only three days before I got a call from the director of the camp, telling me I had to come pick up my son. There had been a fight, a bunk door slamming, a boy being knocked unconscious, Miles running away and hiding in the chapel, the counselors having to look for over an hour to find him. He wasn't welcome at the camp anymore.

I'd been standing in my office at work when I got the call, dressed in a navy-blue pencil skirt and heels, and I'd had to hold on to the desk for support as I got the news. It didn't sound like Miles to start a fight, but boys developed rapidly at that age, and he was in an unfamiliar environment; I supposed anything could happen. I told the director in an unsteady voice that I'd be right there, and in the middle of the day on a Wednesday, I left work to drive three hours into the heart of the Ozarks to collect my bruised and chastened son.

Half an hour into the car ride I lost the only good radio station I could find. It had been mostly commercials anyway, so I reached over and turned the thing off. An uncanny silence deepened around me as trees brushed past, the road narrowed, and I moved further and further away from all that was familiar. As the landscape entered a more wild state, so did my mood.

I'd been about to leave on a long-planned business trip when the camp had called, and this unexpected upending of plans had come at a particularly bad time. Ever since I'd adopted Miles I'd turned down opportunities at work in order to be there for my son, to volunteer at his school and pick him up on early release days, to take him to the doctor and all of his various appointments. I hadn't received a promotion in over ten years because I'd always put Miles first, and always had to. When I signed Miles up for the camp three months earlier, I'd told my boss at work and asked to be given an out-of-town assignment with a new client. To earn any kind of promotion at work outside travel was required, and I wanted to show my boss that I was entering a phase where I could do what he needed me to do. Everything had rested on this being a successful trip, and for weeks I'd researched the clients, worked up a detailed report, even meticulously planned the outfits I'd wear for the various meetings. I was embarrassed to admit how much I'd been looking forward to the mid-rate hotel and company-paid dinners. Staring at the relentless blue sky as I drove deeper into the Ozarks, thinking ahead to two unplanned weeks at home with Miles with no child care or day camps set up, instead of the first two weeks to myself in over ten years, I couldn't help but cry with disappointment. Stupid, fat tears that I didn't bother to stop. Everything flowed in an unhindered release until my phone jarred me out of my self-pity with its vibrating ring.

I answered the call blind, unable to see who it was through my tears and while trying to stay focused on the road. It turned out to be my uncle.

I wiped my eyes with the back of my hand as I listened to him talk. He needed to know if Miles and I were coming to his annual 4th of July party. Every year Uncle Ian hosted a neighborhood BBQ with two smoke pits and beer that spilled with abandon out of the tailgate of his truck. There was usually a lot of smoking, some drugs, and enough fireworks to get somebody in trouble. It wasn't really kid friendly and while we'd gone a few times in the past, I hadn't taken Miles in years.

"Are you crying?" Uncle Ian interrupted himself to ask. There was judgement in his voice.

"No. Yes. Maybe." I grabbed an old McDonald's napkin and tried to wipe my nose, but the scratchiness of it just made me sneeze. I was a mess.

"Why?" he asked, and like an idiot, I spilled the story to him in its entirety. I guess I needed to get it out, I guess I needed someone, anyone, to shoulder it with me, but I should have known better, even in the moment.

"So was it worth it?" he asked when I was done.

"Was what worth it?"

"Adopting that baby. Was it worth the loss of your husband, the loss of your home, the loss now of your career, just to adopt that crack lady's baby?"

When I got to the camp my tears were gone and my face cleaned up. I found my son sitting alone on a wooden bench outside the main dining hall, waiting for me. When he saw me walking towards him he looked down. He didn't jump up, or run to me, or even seem happy to see me. I felt a wave of anger towards him, then a surprising coolness. I sat down on the bench beside him and asked what had happened.

"I hit someone," Miles admitted.

"Ok." I took a breath. "Why?"

Miles shrugged. My usually talkative son was remaining closed-lipped; another change I'd started only recently to notice in him. I tried to get the story out of him from his perspective, but all I could get was a curt repeat of the facts: an argument, a punch, an escape into the chapel. Miles didn't attempt to deflect blame or defend himself in any way.

"What about your friends?" I asked. "Hunter and Josh, where were they? Didn't they stand by you?"

Miles turned his head to the side so I couldn't see the expression on his face, and mumbled something. I was beginning to understand that maybe the boys weren't as close of friends as I'd thought they were.

"C'mon," I finally said, looking out over the treetops of a camp I knew we'd never return to, "let's get out of here." I smiled at Miles and that was when he reached over and hugged me. I kissed the top of his head and inhaled his familiar scent. *So was it worth it?*

* * *

A few days later, Miles and I went to our favorite restaurant for breakfast. Things had started to return to normal at home. We still hadn't talked about what exactly had happened at the camp, but I no longer felt I needed to know. It had been a stupid idea to begin with. Not only was an overnight camp a difficult experience to begin with, but I had sent Miles to a camp of over 300 kids, only a few of which were Black. Whatever had happened, I doubted the place had been that welcoming.

"I'm sorry," I said to Miles. "I never should have sent you to that camp. I just thought you might like it, because your friends were going."

"They aren't my friends."

"I'm starting to understand that."

"Can you teach me how to ride a bike?"

"Oh," I said, nonplussed at the change in topic. I watched as Miles looked to his plate and poured an enormous quantity of syrup over his defenseless, now drowning pancakes. "Sure. It's about time to do that, isn't it?"

"Um, yeah, everybody else knows how to ride but me."

"*Everybody*," I laughed, "that can't be true."

"Actually, it is," Miles said defensively, looking up at me. "There wasn't a single other kid at camp that didn't know how to ride a bike but me. I was the only one." We stared at each other across the table and I realized that I was finally getting a hint of what had happened. I also understood that, on some level, my son had already blamed me for it, for this never-ending not-fitting-in theme of his life. He didn't know how to ride a bike, he didn't have a Brady jersey, he didn't live in a two-story house, he didn't have his father. I'd always assumed that teaching a kid to ride a bike was a father's responsibility, and so of course I hadn't thought to do it, and it hadn't been done.

"I'm sorry, baby, we'll do it this weekend. I promise."

The following Saturday afternoon Miles and I borrowed a bike from one of the neighbors whose kid was still away at camp, and went out onto the streets to learn how to ride. We worked at it for hours, Miles trying, and failing, to balance by himself.

"I can't do it!" he yelled after we'd been at it for more than an hour. A visible frustration stretched every muscle in his tight body.

"You can," I told him calmly. "Try again."

Miles swung a leg over the seat and steadied himself.

"Ready?"

"Ready."

I pushed Miles off, but pretty quickly the bike began to wobble. In his determination to ride already Miles refused to let go, and he steered straight into the curb. He toppled to the ground and I saw blood pour from his knee. I ran to my son and embraced him in a tight hug. The grip of his skinny arms around my sweaty neck as tears fell from both our eyes made everything right again between us.

"I'm sorry baby," I said. "I'm so, so sorry."

The world could be mean and cruel and confusing and difficult but it was never a child's fault. As a mother, you were supposed to be there for them, no matter what. My own mother, and not Uncle Ian, had been right about the most important thing, that there was nothing so great as the love of a mother for her child. It was worth every skirmish, every argument, every disappointment, every loss. It was worth losing a promotion for, it was worth driving across the Ozarks for, and it was certainly worth begging for.

I collected myself. “Uncle,” I said, at last cutting off his harangue, “I don’t need money, but I do need help.”

And my uncle, god bless him, gave me the number of a lawyer to call.

# Chapter 16

"Zame!" an officer called out, and I jumped to attention. I walked quickly up to the partition. "Are you Miles Zame's mother?"

Of course the first person to ever ask me that without a hint of doubt would be a police officer. "Yes."

"How old is he?"

"Sixteen."

"Date of birth?"

"July sixteenth—wait, why do you need that? Are you charging him with something? Are you booking him?" Suddenly I wondered if 'booking' was the right word, or if no one actually used that except on cop shows.

"Just paperwork ma'am. Any history of arrest?"

"No." But the officer had heard me pause. He looked up from his desk and directed his gaze directly into mine. "No," I said again, this time with more confidence. And technically it was true. But that didn't mean he hadn't come close.

"I've called a lawyer," I said. "If you have any other questions you can ask him, when he gets here." I turned before the officer could say anything more and sat back down. I worked to steady my breathing. I was scared. I was really, really scared, in a way that I didn't know it was possible before to be scared.

Like I imagined soldiers felt deep in the trenches in WWII, the bombs flying close, the muck at your feet, a pervasive sinking feeling with the stench of death surrounding you.

I closed my eyes and saw again the frightened look in Miles' eyes the first time he'd been accosted by an authority figure, the time that he was almost arrested. That was it, I suddenly realized, that was the day the change in Miles had happened. If I were to pinpoint a moment to tell my uncle when things had diverged down this darkened path in our lives, it would have to have been then, not the volunteering at the shelter, not the overnight camp, but that day at Wal-Mart. Miles' awareness of his circumstances in life, his out-of-placeness, his uniqueness, his Blackness, had been building and cresting until this was the event that finally tipped him over into another place.

Miles had been twelve years old, and we were in a local Wal-Mart shopping for half-priced chocolate after Valentine's Day. Miles was over five feet tall at that point, and entering the transition I'd been told about from friends like Tiffany, the one I'd been warned to pay attention to, the one where he turned in the eyes of the rest of the world (if not to his mother), from a cute and adorable young boy, into a scary and threatening Black man. I'd been warned about it, but no warnings can really prepare you.

We'd had a good morning that day. We'd slept in, had a large breakfast, and exchanged Valentine's Day gifts - I'd given Miles a Naruto t-shirt, and he'd given me a card with a poem he'd written in school. It was a cold February day, but despite it being the thick of winter, it didn't feel that bad when we got in the car, and streaks of green could be glimpsed beneath the melting snow on the sides of the road as we drove into town.

We'd found a lot of good candy still in stock, and were happily checking out at the register and heading towards the exit, when it happened. My son was lagging behind me, trying to open a bag of individually wrapped Kit-Kats with his teeth. I was walking ahead of him, unawares, tapping on my phone as I strode forward, when a woman popped out of nowhere and abruptly stepped in front of my son.

"You need to return what you stole," she said to him, loudly enough. The automatic doors of the Wal-Mart opened and closed, the ebbing sun of the late winter day flashed blindingly. The few other customers near the exit walked discreetly around us. "What?" my son asked. I slowly put my phone into my back pocket and watched what was happening as if it were a show, not thinking fast enough to get in the middle of it.

A side door I'd never noticed in all my years of coming to Wal-Mart opened, and a uniformed, heavy-set man strode menacingly out of it, up to my son. He grabbed Miles and pushed him towards the secret surveillance room he'd just emerged from. There was no hesitation, no debate, no concern or kindness for a twelve-year-old boy's fear or consternation. There was only barely restrained anger as a large, older white man in uniform grabbed my son and took him away.

"What are you doing?" I yelled, finding my voice. "What is going on?"

"This doesn't concern you," the woman said, blocking my way and trying at the same time to give me some sort of look of common understanding. "We have evidence that this boy stole that candy he was just eating. He walked right past the register with it. We need to question him now."

"*I* paid for that candy," I said. "You do *not* need to question him, you *need* to let him go. Right Now."

The woman looked at me. Seconds ticked past.

"That is my son," I said, as if she were stupid. I tried to get around her, but she moved quickly to block me.

"What the hell are you doing?" My son had just disappeared behind a heavy metal door into a room I'd never seen before with a man I didn't trust. I was ready to knock this woman down if she didn't get out of my way. "Get out of my way," I said, with barely restrained anger. "That is my *son*."

The woman seemed to hear me for the first time. "He's with you?" she asked, perplexed.

"Yes."

"Can I see your receipt?"

I searched frantically through the bag I was holding, imagining the entire time what could be happening to Miles that very minute behind that closed door. Finally, I located the receipt. The woman held it critically before her eyes while many more slow, agonizing seconds passed. Then she turned from me and spoke softly into a walkie-talkie. After what seemed like an interminable minute, the secret door whose outline in the wall I could now discern, opened again. My son emerged, his clothes disheveled, his face distraught. The natural joy in his eyes, the joy of a child, the joy of a boy who knew no injustice, no longer there. I ran to him and hugged him, but Miles was wooden; he didn't hug me back.

I could tell that my son was scared. I attributed his silence to confusion. I spoke a rush of words at him, explaining what had happened while trying to console him, but he didn't hear me – his attention was elsewhere. My son's beautiful brown eyes were blank.

I found out later, much later, that in the moments he was alone with the male security guard, the man had roughly lifted Miles' shirt and pulled down his pants and searched him all over for hidden merchandise. My son had done nothing wrong, and yet he'd been horribly violated, without explanation or apology. He had stolen nothing, while from him was stolen the trust of a child. It didn't escape my son's notice that I'd been *right there*, and yet, I, his mother, the most important person in his life, had been unable to protect him.

My son never went shopping with me again after that, an errand he used to enjoy. And as Tiffany had warned me, the light in his eyes never shone quite so bright again either. The childhood look of curiosity, joy, innocence, and discovery, had been replaced with an adult's look of hesitation, fear, uncertainty, and distrust. And though I tried, I never could get the old cheerfulness back. I hugged him and kissed him, bought him the electric scooter I knew he'd been wanting, told him how much I loved him and how special he was. But all my efforts seemed to do, was make a mother's desperation obvious. My son knew he could no longer trust me to keep him safe. He grew even more reclusive after that, retreated even further from his friends, from me, from everyone around him. I stayed awake at night for weeks after the incident, thinking that my son had finally realized not just the injustice of the world, but that he never should have been given to me in the first place.

# Chapter 17

*A*n hour after I made the call, at 5:57 in the morning, a lawyer walked into the police station. He was on the high side of middle-age, wearied looking, with a worn suit and dilapidated briefcase, but he was white, male, and unafraid of the police. After a quick glance around the waiting area he advanced towards me, unimpressed with everyone else in the room.

"Rachel Zame." He said my name less as a question than as a statement.

I stood up. "Yes."

"Good to meet you." He pumped my hand while looking me up and down. "Your uncle's an old buddy of mine from, well, the less said about that the better. We're here for your son, correct?"

I nodded.

"C'mon." He turned and I followed as the lawyer strode up to the intake desk and banged on the plastic partition with a knuckle. I stepped back, the sound startling, like thunder. I glanced over my shoulder to see if anyone was watching. I was glad to have help, to not be on my own any longer in this horrible place, but the lawyer's confidence was disorienting. I'd always approached the front desk with hesitation, and stood there patiently when I wanted to talk with the officer behind the partition, but there was clearly another way to do things.

"Miles Zame," the lawyer said authoritatively. "I'm here to represent Miles Zame." The officer actually got up from behind his desk and came to stand at the partition. He'd never gotten up for me before. When I sought his attention, he generally raised his head to look at me, but he never bothered to get up off his ass for me.

"Still processing," the officer said, his hands in the air as if processing was a mystery, to him included.

"No statements," the lawyer said. "He doesn't agree to give any statements unless I'm in the room. You got that?"

The officer nodded.

"And, of course, I need to see him as soon as possible." The lawyer turned to me. "How long has it been?"

"Three, maybe three and a half hours already."

"Oh, well, that's nothing," the lawyer said, leaning back and shifting the weight of his feet. "It can easily take four to six." He nodded to the police officer who turned away and sat back down, an unspoken but understood common language passing between them.

"Let's sit," he said, putting his hand on the small of my back. "And you can tell me everything you know."

The lawyer, who insisted on being called Bob, was a tax attorney, not a criminal defense lawyer, but he was available, he'd dabbled in stuff like this before, and he owed my uncle a favor. Besides, he'd recently gotten a divorce, he told me quite freely in conversation, and he had too much time on his hands that needed to be filled anyway. This was better than sitting up all night watching TV in one's underwear. When he said this I had an image that was then difficult to dislodge from my mind.

"My wife left me six months ago," Bob admitted, veering far away from the details of Miles' case. "For a younger man. Usually it goes the other way – the husband cheats on the wife – but not in my case. No, ma'am."

As I listened to the lawyer I nodded, wondering how to bring the conversation back to the topic of my son.

"Right in the middle of a load of laundry—"

"Are you representing both boys?" the officer at the front called out from behind the partition. "Miles Zame and Desmond Harrison?"

The lawyer looked at me and I shook my head. "No," he called back. "Just Miles Zame." Then he turned to me and asked, "Who's Desmond Harrison?"

That was a good question. Who *was* Desmond Harrison? I no longer knew. I don't think I had ever really known. He was the one other Black boy in Miles' class, and he'd shown up in the middle of eighth grade, just a few years before.

It had been early January, the holiday break from school and work had just ended and Miles had returned to the classroom uninspired and unenthusiastic. I had had to bribe him with Reese's peanut butter and chocolate cereal in the morning to get him up, and then yell at him at night to get off his Xbox and into bed. He claimed to do his homework some time in between, but I rarely saw it.

"I know!" Miles yelled, when I told him for the third time that it was time to brush his teeth and get ready for bed. The anger in his voice surprised me, and as I handed him a towel I told him to drop the attitude. But then, bending to pick up his discarded socks, I saw the thin black hairs newly sprouting on his legs. I sized him up and realized how much taller than me he was. I kissed my son good night, missing the days he asked me to stay with him and read him a story.

A couple of weeks into the semester, a smiling Miles returned to me. My son bounded into the car when I picked him up after school one afternoon, and he told me all about this new kid, Desmond. Desmond was tall, skinny, and Black, just like Miles. Desmond was an only child, also like Miles. And Desmond was devoted to Steph Curry and the Golden State Warriors – it was like Miles had found his soul mate. It didn't take long after Desmond's arrival at school for he and Miles to become the best of friends, and for their friendship to displace nearly all of the others Miles had made in the neighborhood over the years. At first, I'd been overjoyed that they'd found each other.

"How's school going?" We were having dinner, and Miles had been answering my questions again, instead of shrugging at everything I said.

"Desmond wants to start a Black Student Union," Miles said. "Just the two of us. Our own BSU." My son laughed out loud and my heart had lifted to see him so joyful.

When summer came a few months later, if Miles wasn't at basketball camp or Desmond away visiting his father in Memphis, the two were inseparable.

"Who are you texting at eight in the morning?" I asked Miles one day as I got ready for work and he emerged from his bedroom, disheveled and sleepy-eyed. I'd long promised Miles a phone when middle school ended and before high school began, and in the very first week of summer he'd made sure I'd gotten him one.

"Desmond," Miles mumbled without looking up.

I watched my son literally walk into a wall as he headed to the bathroom. It took effort not to laugh out loud.

"Can I have ten dollars?" Miles asked when he joined me in the kitchen a few minutes later. "For lunch."

"The fridge is full," I said, pointing towards the refrigerator while pouring Miles a glass of orange juice. "There's lots to eat here."

"I know," Miles said, giving me the sly grin that made me think how handsome he was getting to be. He took the orange juice from me. "But we're going to the rec center to shoot hoops. And hang at the pool. We won't be coming back here."

"Oh, ok. I guess. But don't come home so late again tonight. After dinner is way too late, I get worried. Be here by dinner."

"Sure Mom," Miles said, looking down at his phone again. A minute later he was headed out the front door. I watched my son get on his bike and ride towards the rec center without turning around to wave goodbye.

I tried to get Miles to read some books that summer, or engage in a conversation with me longer than two minutes, but it was a futile effort, and what was summer for when you were young, anyway? I was happy that Miles seemed happy, and that he had finally found a best friend. Everyone should have a best friend, I remembered thinking.

For a while, I'd hoped that Desmond's mother would become my new best friend too. She was a single mother, like me, having gotten a divorce from Desmond's father the year before. She was also a professional, like me, working long hours as a nurse at the local hospital. I thanked god she wasn't one of those wealthy, stay-at-home moms, that littered the neighborhood in the mornings jogging in their too-tight spandex and bouncy pony tails. No, Cierra could be seen shuffling Desmond out of the house they now shared with her parents, harried, annoyed, exasperated, real. She seemed relatable, she seemed like someone I could share a bottle of cheap wine with, someone who wouldn't mind telling an embarrassing story about a bad date. I invited Cierra over for dinner multiple times, but she always turned me down. And I never knew why.

The first time I had any doubts about Desmond was a year after he'd moved to the neighborhood, during Christmas break from school the boys' freshman year of high school. The bank where I worked closed early during the winter holidays, so I was home more than usual, baking cookies and watching old movies on Netflix. I don't know if it was the games on Miles' Xbox, or the latitude I gave both boys to stay up late, but they gravitated to our apartment that holiday, and spent most of their time with me. I remember feeling like the cool parent, the with-it parent, the parent kids willingly chose to tell their secrets to and spend their time with. I imagined it was my amazingly good chocolate chip cookies, which disappeared five minutes after coming out of the oven, that made the boys want to be with me, not my look as an easy mark.

One afternoon, just before Christmas, Desmond came over to our apartment with a present for me. It was the holiday season, after all, so not entirely out of place. Indeed, my initial reaction when Desmond pulled the box out of his backpack and handed it to me was that it was quite thoughtful of my son's best friend to think of me at that time of year. I thanked him for being so considerate. I assumed the rectangular box he handed me held a pen, or a tube of gumballs, or some other trinket a fifteen-year-old boy might think I'd like. I didn't know how to react when I opened it and saw that it contained an intricately braided thin silver bracelet. I stood there, the boys watching me, and it was quiet for a moment before I remembered to thank Desmond. I let him snap the jewelry on my wrist, I listened as he told me how when he had seen it, he knew it would fit me perfectly.

I wanted to call Cierra, but I didn't know if that was the right thing to do. No parent likes hearing suspicions about their child. And unless I knew for certain that the bracelet was stolen, what was the point? I knew Desmond sometimes got beatings from his grandfather, and I didn't want to be the cause of another one of those. I wanted Desmond to trust me. I wanted the boys to keep spending so much of their time at our apartment. When I asked Miles about the bracelet later, he assured me that Desmond's part-time job at the mall paid well, and that he definitely could afford it. I wondered if my son was naïve. I didn't know if my son was lying.

When I thought about it more at night, I had another fear: that I was thinking the worst of Desmond because he was Black. If Miles' best friend had been white, and had shown up with an expensive Christmas present for me, would I have been so quick to wonder if it had been stolen? If I were honest with myself, probably not. If it had been Hunter or Josh or one of Miles' other ivory-white school friends, I probably would have assumed he'd earned the money from a summer job, or been given the money from a rich parent's too-generous allowance. I would have much more easily brushed the incident off, and worn the bracelet with a smile. And because I didn't with Desmond, I was ashamed of myself.

This was a recurring experience for me. Suspecting myself of racial bias, and then being extremely embarrassed by it. A few months before I'd been driving in downtown St. Louis and was stopped at a stoplight when a group of three Black teenage boys approached my car. Immediately, I'd locked the doors and pushed my purse beneath the passenger seat. And then in the very next instant, I noticed the white bucket the boys were carrying, stenciled with the name of a veteran's charity in black ink on the side. I'd been overcome with shame. A red hot shame that actually made my hands shake as they fell into my lap. Had it been a group of white boys, not only wouldn't I have instinctively locked the car, but I was pretty sure I would have smiled and lowered my window instead, calling out to the boys with a $5 donation.

Another time I'd been walking along the sidewalk downtown, and as I passed the corner of a Metro station, I noticed a Black woman standing by the ticketing machine, hunched over, rifling through her purse. I assumed she didn't have enough money to buy a ticket, so I'd stopped and offered her some. She looked up at me curiously, declined the money, and then told me pointedly that she'd actually been looking for her new iPhone, which she was pretty sure now she'd left at home, in her condo, up a few blocks on swanky Lindell Street.

The problem wasn't just that I was embarrassed by these episodes, the problem was that they brought home to me the warning message of that adoption article from years before. I was white, and so didn't understand racism. I was white, and so couldn't relate to the daily life of a Black American. I was white, and so unfit to be a parent to a Black son. The possibility of the truth of these sentiments haunted me. It made me question everything I did, every thought I had, every action I took. It definitely made me not want to question Desmond about the bracelet, or the $19.99 porn film that showed up on our cable bill, or the too-loud music, too-low pants, or anything else for that matter. What did it say about me that I so easily assumed the worst about my son's best friend?

"Desmond is Miles' best friend," I told the lawyer. "He's a good kid."

# Chapter 18

***B***ob looked concerned. The lines above his bushy eyebrows creased inwards as he frowned in thought. “So what are they being charged with?”

“I don’t know,” I exclaimed in exasperation. “No one’s told me a thing. They,” I stuck a thumb towards the front desk, “ignore me every time I go up and ask. That’s why I called you.”

The lawyer stared at me for a second, then got up and rapped on the partition again. “I need to see my client,” he insisted this time. “And I need to know what he’s being charged with.” The officer behind the desk hesitated, then got up and disappeared out a side door. The lawyer turned to me. “Ok. I’ll handle things from here. It’s better that way. You can go get some coffee or something, take a break.”

I looked at the lawyer as if he were crazy. “I’m not leaving.”

Bob sighed with resignation. “When they let me back there,” he nodded towards the door that led to the rest of the station, “I’ll be seeing Miles alone. I’m not sure if you thought you were going back there with me, but I don’t recommend it. I need Miles to feel comfortable telling me anything.”

I opened my mouth, then shut it. *I do too*, I wanted to reply, *I need Miles to feel comfortable telling me anything too.* But I said nothing. I swallowed my feelings. I wasn't even sure who or what I was angry at anymore. The lawyer, for taking over and assuming such a patriarchal attitude, the police, for ignoring me all night, the world, for having dumped my son into this hot fucking mess. I wanted to ask *Bob* what the harm was in seeing my own son, but I knew deep down that he had a point and that I should probably just let him take over for now. I imagined what would happen if I went back there with him; it'd be like the conversations I had with Miles every time he brought home a bad report card. I'd face him across the kitchen table and ask how it had happened, he'd slouch in his chair and clamp his mouth shut, and our mother-son entrenchment would only deepen.

I rubbed the temples on the sides of my head and briefly closed my eyes. Then I watched as a police officer came out into the main waiting area, motioned for Bob to follow him, and then led this lawyer I didn't really know, and only barely trusted, into the back of the station. Into the cold, drab detention area where I imagined my scared, hungry son was nervously waiting.

I eventually walked over to the wall of the police station that was alongside the entrance and opposite the front desk. There was a short, rectangular window in the corner, though I discovered when I approached that it was epoxied shut. I pressed my fingers against its cold metal frame and felt the chill of the glass along my skin. I looked out into the grey sky. I recalled lying in bed with Miles when he was a baby, his body draped along my stomach, his curled fists pressed into my sides. His warmth against mine had been comforting. His smell had been newborn sweet. I remembered looking out the window of that bedroom and thinking: *this is exactly how I want to die.* That moment of maternal contentedness had been pure bliss. I'd wondered how I could preserve it, crawl into it, and never let go of it until my last breath. I had looked down, watching Miles's back lightly rise and fall, the baby blue curtains of the window next to us rustling as the heat in the house kicked on. There had been barely a sound as a few brown leaves on the tree outside desultorily fell to the ground.

A tear slid down my cheek now as I looked out the police station window. All I saw were the amorphous shapes of cars and a desolate parking lot. I could still smell Miles's smell, I could still feel his flesh. My son was a treasure; he was my love, my life, my joy. He gave me headaches sometimes, and lately we'd been fighting all the time, but it was only because we cared so much about each other. Because I loved him enough to fight for his future, and he loved me enough to hate disappointing me. He needed to be free so we could argue another day.

And then I had the sudden, frightening thought: does Miles even know how to act once detained by the police? I know he knew to be calm and deferential when being arrested, but afterwards? What about once you'd already been arrested, and were waiting in the back of the station, did Miles know to keep being deferential even then? Or was he talking back like he did with me, and lately, with his teachers at school? Miles' most recent defiant pose, with his weight thrown back and his arms crossed tightly against his chest, could be quite infuriating. My mind buzzed all over the place, forging ahead into dangerous scenarios I knew weren't good for me to imagine, but which I was unable to stop. Fear traveled along my skin and deep into my heart as I imagined Miles unwittingly making things worse for himself.

The last time I'd tried having The Talk with Miles, about the police and how to behave around them, my son had gotten up in the middle of our conversation and left the room. He'd actually walked out on me. We'd finished dinner and were about to have dessert - Oberweis ice cream with chocolate sprinkles on top, his favorite - and I was getting the spoons out when Miles turned on the television and a news reporter flashed on the screen. A group of Black teenagers had been arrested for leaving a local restaurant without paying the tab. It was the diner where Miles and I had eaten so many of our pancake breakfasts, and played so many of our games of *Which Do You Prefer*. Swarms of police vehicles and flashing lights filled the television screen. My son and I both watched without moving.

When the segment ended I handed a bowl to Miles. "You know you're supposed to do whatever the police tell you to do, right? Even if it seems wrong or unfair, you just do it. You *don't argue.* If the police stop you, you do what they say. Ok?"

"You know they didn't do it," Miles said, indicating the kids on TV. "You know they just got targeted."

Truthfully, I had no idea what had happened. The two-minute clip wasn't enough to tell me if the kids were guilty of something, or not. I'd done stupid things as a teenager, so it was possible, but I'd also been privileged enough as a small white female to get away with most of it. Those kids knew they didn't have such leeway, so Miles was probably right, they hadn't done it; it wasn't worth the chance. I nodded. "Yes, but tell me you know to listen to the police. To always do what they say."

Miles rolled his eyes. "I know."

That was fast becoming my son's favorite phrase. *I know*, as in I know mom, now leave me alone. *I know*, I'm not stupid. *I know*. My son took his bowl from me and left to eat his ice cream in his bedroom. Another conversation between us had ended, before it had really begun.

We'd first had The Talk years earlier, of course. I'd broached the subject when he was still in middle school, when he'd turned thirteen and was growing out of his clothes so fast I couldn't keep up. He was a Black boy tottering on the edge of manhood, and in certain lights and from certain angles he already looked like an adult. Even then, it had been hard to tell if Miles had taken my talk seriously. I wasn't a fellow Black man, who could tell him earnestly and with lived experience how important it was to monitor your behavior, especially around the police. To not make sudden moves. To always sound respectful. To reply with nothing but a 'yes, sir.' I related to Miles stories I'd heard, or read about in the paper, of incidents where things had gone terribly wrong, but I could tell it wasn't the same as sharing the vulnerability with him; it wasn't the same as living the fear.

The next time Tiffany called I asked if she thought her husband could help me. She put Cedric on the line and I admitted that I'd given Miles the talk about authority figures and what to do if stopped by the police, but that I'd thought he hadn't taken it seriously. He needed to hear it from a Black man.

"Yeah, that's about right," Cedric agreed in his deep, bass voice. "But it shouldn't be over the phone. When's the next time you all are coming out here?"

"I don't know," I replied. "As soon as possible?"

"Yeah, that's about right," Cedric said again.

We'd driven out a few weekends later, Miles annoyed at having two days of sleep, hoops, and Xbox interrupted, and I feeling a kind of resignation towards the trip, a sadness that I needed such parenting help. After we got in the car and started the drive, however, my mood lifted. A trip would be good, I thought, Miles might even talk to me on the five-hour drive to Chicago.

Instead, within minutes of hitting the road he'd put his headphones on and proceeded to watch *Rogue One*, and then *Solo*, on his tablet. He thanked me when I bought him skittles and iced tea at the rest stop, and flashed for a second his brilliant smile, but that was all the attention I got.

When we arrived at Tiffany and Cedric's house, on a tree-lined suburb outside Chicago, Miles quickly disappeared with their son Jayden and some kids from the neighborhood. I went inside the house and caught up with my old friend. Tiffany looked good – older, time was wearing us all down bit by bit, but the lines around her mouth and beside her eyes framed a happiness, a contentedness with life that looked handsome on her. I stood by Tiffany in the kitchen and, along with her mother-in-law, rolled biscuits, seasoned chicken, and fried up green beans in bacon fat. There wasn't any danger we weren't going to eat well.

When everyone gathered together around the table for dinner that evening, there were so many people - a quadrupling of the usual me-and-Miles dynamic - that the loudness and the laughter were disorienting. I looked over at Miles but he seemed fine, smiling and stuffing food into his mouth as if he feared its sudden disappearance. When dessert was brought out, a pound cake topped with strawberries and whipped cream, Miles blurted out, "I wish I was here every night!"

It got quiet for a moment and I bent my head in shame.

"No, you don't," Jayden said, rescuing the moment, "'cause if you did you'd have an annoying sister to deal with."

"Hey!" Zariah protested, punching her brother in the arm. The laughter quickly picked up again around the table.

Cedric talked to Miles sometime before bed. I never learned exactly what he said, and I never asked, but the drive back down to St. Louis was very different than the drive up. No feet on the dashboard, no listlessness, barely any attitude. It made me wonder if Cedric had also talked to Miles about respecting one's mother. Miles sat straight up in the seat next to me, his seat belt tight around him without my having to ask him to put it on. His backpack was settled neatly on the floor beside his feet, clearly visible from the side window. Ten minutes into the drive he asked if I had a copy of his birth certificate.

"Your birth certificate? Sure, somewhere. Why?"

"Until I get a driver's license, we need some sort of ID for me. And we need to keep it in the car, or in your purse, somewhere easily accessible."

"Ok."

"So if we get stopped I can prove who I am, that I'm your son, that I'm still a minor."

I looked over at Miles and nodded.

"And you need to clean this thing up," he said, indicating the fast-food bags still littering the back seat from our drive up. "Everything makes an impression, mom. Everything."

"You're right," I agreed, nodding.

While I never learned exactly what was said between Cedric and Miles, I realized now, waiting in the drab police station, that I'd always assumed it was enough.

I turned away from the window and sat back down on the wooden bench in the middle of the waiting area. I leaned over and put my head in my hands. The tendrils of a migraine tickled the back of my neck. I reminded myself that I knew that Miles was physically ok. I had heard his voice and I knew, at least, that he hadn't been shot. But that bit of truth didn't hold as much comfort as one would have thought. Sandra Bland had died *in* jail, in police custody, not outside it. And what exactly *was* the protocol after you were arrested, after the police detained you and you were waiting to prove your innocence? Had Cedric talked to him about that too? I felt a desperate need to see my son. I ached to look into his eyes, touch his skin, to gather him into my arms. I am his mother, I thought, I deserve to know what is happening. I ought to be in the room.

# Chapter 19

*T*he lawyer emerged from the back of the police station at 6:37 a.m. I could tell from the deepening tracks on his face that the news was bad. He walked slowly towards me, as if encumbered with a heavy weight.

"Tell me more about this girl Sarah," he said, dropping into a chair beside me, like a stone to the bottom of the ocean.

I turned to this stranger who'd been lucky enough to lay eyes on my precious son and asked, "How's he doing? Is Miles ok?"

The lawyer cracked a smile, as if only just remembering that he was talking to his client's mother. "Your boy is fine," he said. "Worried - he's not sure what they're going to charge him with - but physically ok. He's also innocent. At least, he says he's innocent," the lawyer added, interjecting his own doubts, if no one else's.

"What happened? Why are they holding him?"

"They've got him on assault, at least. And maybe rape."

"*Rape?*"

The lawyer nodded. "There was some party. Parents out of town. Things got out of hand. The police were called and Miles was found up in a room with this girl Sarah. She says she was raped."

I opened my mouth, then shut it. There was no way my son had raped anyone. No Way. It wasn't just that he was a sensitive boy, a kind boy who naturally paid attention to other people and easily put himself in their shoes, but more than that, I had not raised him that way. I had read books to my son about famous women and their contributions to society. We had watched movies about suffrage and the early battles women faced in order to have their voices heard. When I bought Miles a puzzle in first grade, of all the U.S. presidents, it was he who turned to me after putting it together and asked, "Where are the girl presidents?" My son witnessed my daily struggle as a single mother. He admired Desmond's mother's strength and vigilance. There was *no way* he could do such a thing.

Especially not to Sarah.

Those two had a history. It was true, she'd turned him down after he asked her to the homecoming dance the year before, but it was also true that they were still friendly with each other. I'd seen them smile when they passed each other on the street, and I knew they sometimes texted each other. Miles had known Sarah for years, since we'd first moved to the neighborhood, and he adored her. He would never harm her.

"It's not true," I breathed to the lawyer.

"Well, yes, your son says the same thing. About the rape. But he admits to the assault."

The words hurt to hear. I tried to picture my son hitting someone. Who would he have gotten in a fight with? And when did my son learn how to throw a punch? I'd certainly never taught him. If this lawyer knew my son, he'd be as incredulous as I was about these charges. Besides, the more I thought about it, the more I realized how little sense it all made. Miles and Desmond never went to the neighborhood parties because, frankly, they were never invited.

The year before there had been a house party on the street behind our apartment, with what seemed like half the high school in attendance – you could hear the music and commotion blocks away – but not Miles and Desmond. They'd gone and walked by the party when we'd all first heard the strains of music filtering over the night air, but the boys had returned within thirty minutes, shaking their heads and making jokes about the terrible music choices. I asked if they didn't want to stay and be with the other kids at the party.

"Nah," Miles said, glancing at Desmond. "We were invited to a party like that once, last year. But we found out it was only 'cuz they thought we'd bring drugs. When we showed up with nuthin, they were actually kind of pissed at us."

I looked at my son, then at Desmond, then back at my son. And then we had all devolved into laughter. We'd needed Kleenex, in fact, to wipe the tears off our faces. For once, I'd been grateful for the stupidity of racism.

"There's no way they were even *at* that party," I said to the lawyer, "let alone beating anyone up at it. Miles and Desmond don't go to the high school house parties."

The lawyer glanced at me sideways. "Well, this time it appears that they did."

I could tell that the lawyer was reevaluating my relationship with my son. The levers in his brain were clicking and pushing up signs labeled "ignorant mother," "stupid woman," and "unhelpful family member." I didn't want to lose his attention, so I started rambling.

"My son's a good kid, you have to understand. It's been hard in this neighborhood, with few kids who look like him, no role models for him to identify with. Basically, no other Black men. I do my best. We talk all the time. I try to make sure we always eat dinner together. He told me himself that he never even gets invited to those kinds of parties. The white kids only expect drugs out of him and Desmond, and they don't do drugs."

The lawyer nodded, but stayed quiet.

"What about Desmond?" I asked. "What's he being charged with?"

"Marijuana possession," the lawyer said, deadpan.

Nothing made sense anymore. I knew the boys didn't do drugs, be it pot, or anything else for that matter. *I'd* recently gotten some medical marijuana on the suggestion from my doctor that it might help with my migraines, but it hadn't, and my son had only lectured me afterwards on smoking's deleterious effects on a healthy pair of lungs. He'd brought back memories of my mother and her lung cancer and her slow and painful deterioration, and I hadn't smoked again since. I'd never smelled pot in his bedroom, or seen it, not once. The boys certainly never acted high. And they'd never been caught with drugs at school, or anywhere else for that matter.

And then my next thought was, how did Desmond end up with the lesser charge?

I imagine there comes a moment in every parent's life when you realize, with a starkness that's as bright and painful as a glance upwards towards a harsh summer sun, that you do not know your child at all. You may have raised him and fed him and loved him and laughed with him, but you still do not have a clue the ideas that run through his mind. You have no idea how he behaves when you are not around. You have no clue how he talks to other people, what jokes he laughs at, what insults he abides. Your child could be a stranger you wouldn't even recognize from behind. I shivered at the realization. It was like looking down on a hike and finding your footing unstable, the ground beneath your feet dark with a soft, dank soil that was failing to hold your weight. I felt myself sinking now, the ground coming up fast.

"What are we going to do?" I asked the lawyer.

"I'm not sure yet," he said, shaking his head. "But you need to tell me more. What did you think your son was doing last night? Where did you think he was?"

# Chapter 20

***I*** had thought Miles was at Desmond's house, that it was like any other night and that the boys were just hanging out playing video games. After dinner Miles had told me he was going to Desmond's to check out the new Spider-Man release on PlayStation. Sometimes on a Saturday night the boys had to work – Desmond at his job at the mall, Miles at the cinema where he sold popcorn and candy – but if they weren't working their jobs the boys were spending time together at Desmond's house or our apartment. I'd told Miles as he'd grabbed his jacket and backpack not to stay out too late, and he'd given me a nod and a smile – an actual genuine smile – before heading out the door. I'd assumed it was just two best friends hanging out together, nothing to be worried about.

Miles had pretty much stopped spending time with his other friends. After Desmond moved to the neighborhood Miles still saw Hunter, Josh, Carson, and the rest of them once in a while, if they found themselves together at the basketball courts after school, or online in games of Fortnite or Apex Legends, but in the last year even those interactions had occurred less and less often, and when I would ask Miles about one of his old friends he'd just shrug and tell me they did other things now. They didn't have jobs, like Desmond and Miles, they joined clubs, like chess and yearbook. Yearbook was quite popular, in fact – I heard from one of the other mother's that nearly everyone wanted to be on the yearbook committee, so they could get as many of their own pictures in the yearbook as possible. When I asked Miles about it, however, he insisted that he didn't want to join. He said he *didn't* want his face plastered throughout the school yearbook, that he hated seeing even his single standard class picture in there.

"Why?" I asked, surprised, knowing that he liked posting Tik Tok videos and seeing himself captured in other ways. "You're the handsomest kid in the class," I added.

Miles sighed. "I don't want to be the diversity poster child for the school." And then he'd admitted to me that he actually ducked and hid every time he saw a yearbook person in a classroom with a camera.

"I get it," I said, not trying to talk him out of avoiding the camera.

I was pretty certain it had just been Miles and Desmond hanging out together the night before, and no one else, but I didn't know exactly what they'd been doing. "They were at Desmond's," I told Bob, "I'm sure of that. Probably playing video games."

"How might they have ended up at that party?" the lawyer pressed me.

I thought about it. Neither of the boys had a driver's license, but Desmond did have a learner's permit and I knew that he had snuck out in his grandfather's car in the past. I'd seen him backing out of the driveway before, when Cierra was working an overnight shift at the hospital and his grandparents were presumably already asleep in bed. I never said anything. I didn't want to be the one to get Desmond into trouble. I supposed the boys could have taken the car and driven by this party, hoping to catch a glimpse of things, maybe even see Sarah or some other girl. I guess I could see them doing that, driving by the party if Miles or Desmond had been interested in someone who they knew was going to be there. It had taken awhile, longer than I'd expected frankly, but my son had at last become preoccupied with girls.

It had started, in some sense, in fifth grade when the school sent an announcement home that there would be a three-week health class on the topic of puberty, and boys' and girls' anatomy. We were advised as parents to prepare our kids for the lesson and talk to them about sex and their changing bodies.

After getting the announcement I'd tried doing that, making Miles' favorite meal for dinner and asking him if he had any questions about girls' or boys' bodies, or how babies were made. But at the time all he'd done was shake his head and push some food around on his plate.

I kept at it, however, wanting to keep the lines of communication open, trying to make sure Miles was comfortable coming to me with any questions he had about sex and the human body. Throughout middle school I asked Miles if he liked any of the girls in his classes, or any of the boys for that matter, but for years he gave me a disgusted look while shaking his head. Sometimes he admitted to me who Josh liked, or who Hunter had tried to kiss at recess, *other* kids who were indeed talking about penises and holes and finding squirreled away moments to show each other things. But Miles himself, through sixth and even seventh grade, insisted it was all gross.

But by eighth grade Miles had finally started bringing up the topic himself, albeit indirectly, through jokes he'd heard or confusing videos he'd seen on YouTube.

"Why do you have to drag a girl by the hair, and not by the feet?" he asked me one day, looking up from his tablet.

"Um, you don't have to drag a girl at all, I don't think."

"Just answer the question, mom."

"Seriously though, that's a terrible question. Never drag a girl anywhere."

"*Ok*, but if you did, why by the hair?"

I sighed. "I don't know. Why?"

"Because if you drag her by the feet, her hole will fill up with dirt."

It was such a terrible joke I didn't know what to say at first. But then it dawned on me that, despite what some of his friends might be doing, Miles had clearly still not seen an actual vagina, and that he had no clue how they worked. "The vagina isn't a gaping hole," I'd finally responded. It won't just fill up with dirt. It's got lips. Is your mouth always hanging wide open?"

But then Miles' mouth did hang open. "A girl's hole has *lips*?"

* * *

By high school, Miles' interest in girls was full blown, blotting out nearly everything else – 2K, Nike Airs, basketball even – nothing consumed him as much as his interest in, and confusion about, girls and what they did.

I found Miles watching the Kardashians on his tablet one afternoon. It didn't seem like the kind of show a teenage boy would watch. I leaned over his shoulder to see what was going on, but he moved to block the screen from my view.

"Is that *Keeping up with the Kardashians*?" I asked.

Miles just glared at me in a way that said *Leave me alone, Mom.* When I remained standing where I was he took the tablet to his bedroom, and closed the door. A few days later I saw him watching *Save the Last Dance*, and then *Candy Jar*, movies that all featured interracial couples.

I considered Sarah. She was white, and beautiful, like a lot of the girls in the shows Miles had been watching. Had Miles and Desmond cruised by that party hoping to catch a glimpse of her? But Miles had been friends with Sarah for as long as I could remember, she wasn't a mystery to him. In fourth grade, Sarah was the neighborhood girl who collected Pokémon cards, wore superhero t-shirts, and knew the names of all the Lego Ninja minifigures. All the boys thought she was cool and by middle school they were all comfortable enough around her to let her join their games of pick-up basketball; the only girl who ever did.

Sarah wasn't just a tomboy, however. Over the years she'd grown lanky and tall, with brown hair that swung in waves down the middle of her back. She had big brown eyes and a disarming smile and, frankly, she was gorgeous. When freshman year of high school started I was overjoyed when Miles worked up the gumption to ask her to the homecoming dance. I was as let down as he was when she said no. Despite my prodding, Miles refused to ask anyone else to the dance that year, and instead he stayed home.

Desmond didn't end up going either, having been turned down by both the girls he asked.

"White girls," I overheard Desmond saying to Miles one evening as they sat in Miles' bedroom, "they think they so much better than us. They think they can like our music, like our clothes, flirt with us and tease us, but never actually go out with us. It's bullshit."

I was so surprised by the anger in Desmond's voice I'd nearly tripped. Had Desmond sounded more innocent, more hurt, I would have entered the bedroom and spoken to them about girls and relationships. Instead, I'd backed away down the hall, hoping they hadn't heard me, stalling for time to think.

I contemplated whether I should talk to the boys about dating myself, or have someone who wasn't white do it. I thought of Cedric, but knew that he was busy because Tiffany was out of town again on another international business trip. Her career had really taken off, and she was rarely in the country anymore. I was happy for her, but sad for myself. These were the perils of relying so much on a single close friend. I wished, again, that Cierra and I were better friends. But we weren't.

Unable to sleep one night I'd turned to Facebook. I'd opened my computer and in the blue glow of light typed, "answers to ignorant white questions about inter-racial dating," but no relevant page turned up. I tried, "I have a Black son with a crush on a white girl. What now??" A few edited searches later I came across an inter-racial adoption support group open to new members that had some recent relevant activity. When I read through the threads, however, I noticed one white person after another being hounded for, and made to feel embarrassed by, their basic questions. It was not a welcoming atmosphere. I sighed and closed the computer.

I thought about my mom, something I'd been doing a lot lately as my relationship with Miles entered the rocky teenage years, and I wondered what she would say. She had stressed to me when I started dating to be careful – to keep my guard up in any interaction, even if I already knew the boy. It had been sound advice for me, but it wasn't relevant to my son.

I decided that I just needed to be there, that I needed to make it clear to both Miles, and Desmond, that I was available, no matter the situation. I decided that if I kept the communication lines open, both boys would eventually talk to me. So I baked chocolate chip cookies, I walked noisily down the hall, and I waited, while Miles and Desmond huddled behind Miles' now always closed bedroom door, playing loud music and saying things I could no longer hear.

Thinking about it in the police station, I realized that waiting might not have been the best decision. Miles had not come to me with a question, or even a joke, in months and I suddenly realized that I no longer knew what he was thinking, or, apparently, what he was doing.

"He was with Desmond last night," I said to Bob, holding up my hands. "That's all I know. I thought they were just hanging out playing video games. I honestly don't know anything else."

# Chapter 21

*A* few minutes later, at 6:54 a.m., Cierra burst into the police station. She was still in her hospital scrubs and looked not just disheveled, but disoriented, panic streaked across her face. Cierra was usually rather put together, hair done up tight in a bun, clothes neat and pressed, expression impenetrable. But now her blue nurse's uniform was stained and crumpled, and dark strands of hair stuck up at odd angles from the back of her head. She looked frantically around the waiting area, and when she spotted me, she ran to me and gripped me in a hug. We'd never hugged before, and the contact surprised me.

"How long have they been in there?" she asked, pulling back.

"All night."

Cierra glanced at her watch. "I was on shift, I didn't know. My phone doesn't always ring in the hospital. Why are they holding them? What happened?"

I told her what little I knew. She seemed as suspicious as I was, and the comradery was heartening. I was grateful to finally have a real ally. Cierra let go my hands, nodded politely to Bob after I introduced him, and then approached the front desk. She stood there, talking through the plastic partition to one police officer after another, pointing fingers, engaging them enough so they approached her from behind the desk and talked directly to her. I was impressed. She seemed to be making more headway in ten minutes than I had in three hours.

I closed my eyes, the tendrils of a migraine continuing to lengthen behind my eyes, and prayed it wouldn't blossom and take hold before I saw my son again, before we were able to get Miles and Desmond both out of this place and back home.

I opened my purse and stuck my hand inside, hoping to find a loose ibuprofen or Xanax tablet. I knew it was basically empty, but I rooted around anyway, letting my fingers probe the dry pockets and lint-filled corners. My heart lifted when I brushed past something hard, though I quickly realized it was much too large to be a pill. I tugged on whatever it was until it came loose from the fold of pocket it was tangled up in. My breath caught when I saw that it was the brown-haired, mini-skirted Lego minifigure that was supposed to be me.

I suddenly couldn't keep the tears in any longer. I pictured the desk in Miles' bedroom, the last place I could remember seeing this minifigure, but there were no Legos there now – the room had become a teenager's bedroom, with loose change strewn across the desktop, basketball shoes abandoned on the floor, an unmade bed with the impression of Miles' long limbs stamped in the covers. That was where Miles was supposed to be. His bedroom was where he should have ended up last night.

Bob handed me a Kleenex and I stepped to the side to get a hold of myself. Miles was the most important person in my life. I couldn't imagine my days without him. After Nate left, Miles had taken his place for me in so many ways. He'd become my food taster when I experimented with dishes in the kitchen, he was my judge when I tried on new outfits for work, he was my hiking companion on trails around St. Louis. Hiking was how Miles and I had stayed connected in recent years, even as things got rough between us. Something about the open air, the rustling trees, the delight of a new path, could bring us back together after weeks of adolescent distance. This past summer we'd driven out to Elephant Rocks State Park, to hike the couple of trails there among the tall, rounded boulders. We'd packed gorp and granola bars and two bottles of water each. The ground had been smooth, for the most part, though an exposed tree limb winding across one of the paths had tripped me up early on. We talked little as we moved forward, communicating with the occasional grunt or hand gesture. At the end of the second trail we rested side by side on a bench, drinking water and observing the other hikers as they made their way back to the parking lot.

"Why didn't you have another kid?"

I'd been gazing at a brown and blue butterfly that had landed on the bench beside me, watching its wings open and shut languidly, and was unprepared for the seriousness of Miles' question. For years when Miles was younger he had asked for a little brother, or sister. He'd wanted a companion, a ready playdate, a captive audience for his games and stories. I shifted on the bench and gave Miles the answer I'd always given him before. "Because you were perfect. There was no need for another child."

This time, however, Miles snorted and looked away. I looked at my son's profile, the smooth skin, the strong, defiant jaw.

"We wanted another child," I admitted, "but, to be honest, kids are a lot of work. And your father and I didn't have any help. Most people have their parents, or a sister or an aunt, someone who can come over and at least take care of the laundry. We really could have used that. We didn't know what we were doing in the beginning. I kept losing your binkies, we'd run out of diapers, the house was a total mess, and no one could remember to run the dishwasher so your bottles never seemed to be clean when we needed them." I was trying to be funny, describing the utter chaos of those first few weeks after we'd brought Miles home, but my description was falling flat. Miles was looking at me now, but he still wasn't smiling.

"We did talk about it, your father and I," I said, clearing my throat, "when you were a year or so old. Just after your adoption was formalized, we talked about doing it again. But my parents, as you know, are both gone and your dad's parents live in Florida and don't travel. It just seemed like it'd be too much for us."

Miles looked away from me again.

"It's my biggest regret," I added. "You would have made a great big brother. I wish we could have given you a little brother, or sister, I do. I'm sorry."

"It's just so unfair," Miles blurted out. I noticed that he was crumpling and uncrumpling a granola bar wrapper, and I reached over and steadied his hand.

"What's unfair?"

"My life. It's so totally unfair."

Miles had been using that word a lot since high school had started – unfair. The internet wasn't working and it was unfair. The Doritos bag was empty and it was unfair. A favorite sock was missing and couldn't be found and it was totally unfair. "What do you mean?" I asked.

Miles threw his hands in the air. "Out of all of us my life is the most unfair. Think about it. I never knew my birth parents. Yours is next, I guess, 'cause you lost your parents, though at least you got to know them first. Dad's isn't unfair at all. Grandma and grandpa are still alive in Florida. He gets to see them whenever he wants."

"That's true."

"I'll never get to know who they were. For all I know, I even have brothers, and sisters, like that family that just walked by," Miles said, waving a hand to where a family of six had recently walked past us on their way to their minivan. "I could have a lot of cousins for all I know. I just don't know. There's no way to know."

I moved closer to my son and wrapped my arms around him in a hug, even though he rarely let me do that any longer. After a minute, he relaxed into my embrace. "No," I said to Miles, "you've got it wrong. Your father is the unlucky one, and I'm the luckiest one of us all. Because I have you. Because I get to have you in my life every single day."

When I returned to my seat after getting my tears under control, I found that Cierra had somehow talked her way into getting Desmond out of detention. She was standing near the back detention door, arms folded across her chest, Bob standing next to her. Before anyone could explain to me how this had happened, the large metal door clicked and we all turned and watched Desmond emerge from the back of the station, tentative, frightened, more childlike than I had ever seen him. He stepped forward and fell into his mother's arms.

My heart ached as I watched them. A wave of jealousy swept over me. I'd been waiting all night, for hours at that point, when would I get to see my son? I felt hot, then cold, then hot again. I knew I was unhinged after a night of no sleep and constant worry.

The warm maternal feelings from my memories of just minutes before disappeared and I suddenly felt, watching Desmond and Cierra, that I was a terrible mother; that I must not deserve to have my son back. Sure, Miles and I had companionable hikes sometimes on a Sunday morning, but much more often, we had infuriating, bitter arguments.

"Why are there dishes in the sink, Miles? Go do the dishes."

"Uh-huh, I will."

"Now, Miles, go do the dishes now."

"In a second," Miles said, not moving from his spot on the couch.

"Miles!"

"Just because you want it done, doesn't mean it has to be done *right now.*"

"Actually," I said, my voice rising, "it does. Besides, I've asked you three times already. Had it been done when *I* wanted it done, it would have been done after we finished eating, an hour ago. Get up off your ass, and do the damn dishes."

"Geez, Mom," Miles grumbled, looking at me as if I were a crazy person. "You don't have to yell at me like that."

Later that evening Miles came to me with a video he'd found on YouTube, of a pimple-faced teenager in baseball cap and headphones, explaining to the camera how parents just didn't understand that you couldn't pause a game, that it was, like, interactive. Parents just didn't get how things were nowadays.

I snatched Miles' tablet out of his hands, and threw it in the trash.

That was just days after a blowout we'd had over homework, which Miles never seemed to find important enough to complete. I often found his math worksheets or his book reports crumpled up at the bottom of his backpack, torn, half completed, treated with something bordering contempt.

"You can do better than this," I'd said, holding up his mangled papers.

Miles had shrugged, and turned away from me.

"You need to at least try, Miles. Why don't you even try? You can do this."

"No," Miles had said, "I can't."

"Of course you can."

"I can't."

And we had stared at each other in something of a stand still.

"I'm not like you," Miles said. "Not like that," he quickly added when I looked exasperated, "like school. I don't like school, and I'm not good at it."

Perhaps because the words had been hard to hear, I'd ignored them. Instead of saying something sympathetic, I'd shook my head dismissively and told Miles he could do it, that he was like me and that he just needed to try harder.

I stood still in the station as it sunk in that I was a horrible, nagging, mean mother who clearly didn't deserve her son back.

Desmond walked over to where I stood. Before I could say anything he grabbed me and hugged me as if I were his other mother.

"I'm sorry Mrs. Z," Desmond said after a moment. "I never wanted to go to that stupid party in the first place. It wasn't my idea."

I pulled away from the embrace and nodded.

"We never should have split up. It's like in those horror movies, when you're yelling at the dudes not to split up, but then, they do. We did that. I can't believe we did that. My gramps is always telling us to stick together, but I didn't listen to him. I'm sorry. I never should have let Miles go up those stairs alone."

"It's ok," I whispered, with the little voice I could control. "How is he though?" I asked, clearing my throat. "How is Miles?"

"He's a'right. The police got him on trumped up charges though. He's pissed. He's worried. He's scared."

"Can you tell us what happened?" Bob asked, stepping forward.

"I already told the cops. I told them they was making a mistake, that Miles had been with me, that we were together the whole night, but they wouldn't listen to me."

"It's ok," Bob said, "we'll listen to you. Do you mind?" Bob asked, turning to Cierra. "If I talk to your son and ask him a few questions? It might be helpful."

Cierra nodded, and the three of them stepped outside to talk in private. I found that I couldn't go with them. I was suddenly too weary to stand up any longer; I thought I might fall if I didn't sit down. I sank into a nearby chair and steadied my breathing while *My son is innocent* played on a loop in my head.

# Chapter 22

*W*hen Desmond, Cierra, and Bob came back into the station a few minutes later I was under control. I greeted them with a small smile and Desmond related to me his version of events. They had indeed been at his house playing video games, just like I'd thought. And then around midnight they'd gotten bored and, after checking to make sure his grandparents were asleep and his mom still at the hospital, they'd gone cruising in his grandparents' car, just as I thought might have happened.

They'd had no intention of going to the party. The boys knew about it, of course - the whole school knew about it - but as I'd told Bob earlier, Desmond and Miles never felt comfortable at school parties because they always felt out of place. They knew they stuck out and if anything bad happened, they knew they'd be blamed, which according to Desmond is exactly how things went down.

"We weren't going to go, I swear," Desmond reiterated. "We were driving down Delmar, checking out Milano's and Puzzle's. It was kind of quiet, actually, for a Saturday. Everyone was at that party." Desmond shrugged like I knew what he was talking about, and I nodded. "When Miles' phone rang, we thought it was you, to be honest."

It should have been me, I thought.

"But it was Sarah." Desmond shook his head, as if still in disbelief. "It didn't make sense that she was calling. You know, 'cause they have history and all." Desmond looked embarrassed, like maybe he'd said too much.

"Yes, I know. Miles asked her to homecoming and she turned him down."

Desmond nodded, and then continued. "I didn't hear what she said. We were rocking some XXXtentacion, but Miles looked upset when he got off the phone. He told me to turn around and go to the party."

"But why?" I asked.

Desmond shrugged. "I don't know. I didn't ask. My boy tells me to go somewhere, we go."

Desmond made it sound like Miles called all the shots, when in my mind, it was usually Desmond that was in charge. I shifted my weight on my feet. "You didn't press him?"

Desmond shook his head and held up empty hands. "I just turned around and we headed to the party. Like I said, the music was too loud to do much talking anyway. I knew where to go – everyone at school had been talking about the party for days – and it didn't take us long to get there. The only problem was that when we did, there was nowhere to park." Desmond looked over at his mom and she returned a steady stare. "I told Miles we should just leave, but he said we couldn't. He said we *had* to go in."

I felt myself getting angry at Desmond for blindly driving to this party and not asking Miles any questions about why they were going. I couldn't understand why he hadn't argued his best friend out of it. What had Sarah possibly said to make Miles want to go at all?

"Miles got out while I looked for a spot. He said he couldn't wait. He said it was important." Desmond shook his head, as if he still didn't understand. "That was our first mistake – splitting up. I knew it was wrong at the time, and I didn't want to do it, I swear Mrs. Z, but there was nowhere to park and Miles insisted." Desmond took a breath and his mom reached over and put a comforting hand on his shoulder. "I couldn't just leave gramps' car anywhere."

Desmond was looking for absolution from me, for some sort of forgiveness, and I had to dig deep to give it. I nodded and Desmond continued.

"Miles went in without me. I don't know much about what happened after that. I eventually found a place to leave the car and went in after him, but I'd lost him by then. The party was insane. People everywhere. It wasn't just our high school either, there were dudes there I'd never seen before. When I got past the front door I spotted Miles, but he was already headed up the stairs. I called to him, but he couldn't hear me. He went on without me." As he said this Desmond's voice, surprisingly, broke.

"It's ok," Cierra said to her son.

"Why didn't you go after him?"

"I couldn't. That's what I'm telling you. It was crazy in there. I knew it would be better to just wait by the door. That way when Miles was ready to leave I'd be there – he wouldn't have to search to find me. So I stood just inside the house – easy pickings for when the police showed up – and hoped Miles would come back soon."

"How'd you get arrested on a drug charge?" I asked, accusation involuntarily tinging my voice.

Desmond rolled his eyes. "It happened so fast. Someone called the cops and when everyone realized they'd shown up, it was mass panic. People were screaming and pushing to get out. Before I knew what was happening, Carson had come up behind me and was stuffing his hand down my pants, trying to hide his bag in my underwear."

"Carson did what?"

"He was getting rid of his stash. In my pants. Of course he would choose me." Desmond shook his head, and his mom nodded.

I turned to Bob. "They're framing our boys. That's what they do at that school, frame our boys for everything that goes wrong."

"Like when they got suspended last year," Cierra added. "They didn't even start that fight, yet they were the ones that got suspended."

I nodded in agreement, and Bob looked from one to the other of us.

"What happened last year?" he asked. "Tell me everything."

# Chapter 23

*T*hey'd started high school last year, is what happened, and the transition hadn't been smooth. Miles had never been a star pupil – his interests and passions lay outside the classroom - but he'd never been a troublemaker before high school either. He'd been an active child with too much energy and little focus, but he'd never hurt anyone or teased anyone enough for me to get a phone call from the principal. Sometimes Miles came home and told me about the other kids – Carson, who used to bite people, and Hunter, who went through a kicking phase – but it was always other kids with the aggressive tendencies, and I was forever grateful it wasn't Miles at the center of these incidents.

I was wholly unprepared, therefore, when my son embarked upon his own disciplinary track in high school. It was a narrow lane I had to learn to navigate, between accepting criticism of my child, while also standing up for his interests. The first time the principal phoned me his voice was kindly, and he assured me within seconds that Miles was not hurt, and that he wasn't calling due to an accident. Then he cleared his throat and said he was, however, concerned.

"Concerned about what?"

"The bullying."

"Whose bullying my son?"

"No." The principal seemed as surprised as I was. "Your son is bullying other kids."

"Miles?" I asked.

"Yes. There's been some name calling and inappropriate epithets. I want to remind you that we have a zero-bullying policy in this school. I'm going to have to issue a warning."

"To my son?"

"Yes. To–," the principal paused to shuffle through some papers, "Miles Zame."

"Ok. What does this mean?"

"It means we're opening a file. Three warnings and a student gets suspension. More suspensions after that, and it can lead to expulsion. But we're nowhere near that yet," the principal said, fake laughing. "I'm just laying out the rules, so you understand them. I find it important to alert parents early. But we can all take a breath right now. Just have a talk with your son, ok?"

I tried to get more of the story out of the principal before he hung up. Who else was involved, what words exactly were used, what part my son played, but the principal refused, or seemed unable, to divulge the details. He had called merely to give us a warning.

After the call ended, I thought about it and had to agree that Miles' language could be pretty salty. I had never cracked down on swear words very hard – they were just words, and who cared if you used them once in a while? I'd listened to a podcast once that even claimed that using swear words gave you strength. But perhaps Miles had taken my leniency and run too far with it. I supposed maybe it was time for a talk.

* * *

A few months later the school called again. This time, there'd been a prank. A locker broken into, a dead mouse, a not very funny joke. It didn't sound like Miles, but at the same time, I couldn't be absolutely certain. I told the principal he needed to tell me exactly what had happened, but it turned out he didn't know exactly what had happened, none of the adults did and the kids weren't talking. He merely had his suspicions.

As high school rolled forward, things continued to deteriorate down this clouded, bumpy path. There were more scuffles, pranks, and disruptions; Miles got a second warning. Every time I got a call from the school I was asked if there was something going on at home, if there had been a change they should know about. I bristled at this indirect blame and assured the principal or counselor or whoever had called that our family life was fine, that nothing had changed, that I was still there for Miles and we still ate dinner together every night, and no, the divorce wasn't recent, it had been years ago.

I started to question the instincts of the people in charge. Did the principal see my boy as a young, malleable fifteen-year-old, needing just a bit of guidance, or did he see him as a dangerous, threatening adolescent that ought to be taught his place? If I'd learned anything over the past fifteen years, it was that you could never tell what people were actually thinking, which ones were racist and which were actually compassionate. Sadly, I no longer believed that you could assume the best in people.

By the end of Miles' freshman year, the principal had dispensed with any kind of introductory kindness at all when he called, and skipped straight to the negative behavior he was concerned about.

"There was an incident in the cafeteria."

"What sort of incident?"

"A fight."

"Is Miles ok?"

"Yes, Miles is."

"And?"

"Miles started the fight. He hit a classmate."

"So you say."

"This is his third warning, Mrs. Zame. You need to come get him."

When I arrived at the school later that afternoon to collect my son, I found him and Desmond slumped on a couple of chairs in the waiting area outside the principal's office. Miles looked more bored than alarmed. Desmond looked resigned. My son smiled when he saw me and jumped up, eager to get out of the building. I asked Desmond if he needed a ride home, but he shook his head.

"Later Nigga," Desmond called out after the paperwork had been completed and we were headed out the door. I flinched.

"Later," Miles replied.

It was an overcast day, and a sharp wind snapped at our backs as Miles and I walked to the car. "I'm hungry," Miles said. "Can we go to McDonald's?"

I realized right then that I'd been too lenient with Miles, and for far too long. "Is that all you've got to say?"

"Um, yeah. You know they're overreacting, right?"

"Do I? You just got suspended. From. School. You're telling me you've got *no* responsibility here? None at all?"

"I didn't do anything, Mom, I swear. Nothing wrong, at least."

Miles' nonchalance tipped me over the edge. "Miles! Why can't you understand that school is important? That respecting your teachers and learning from your teachers is important? That keeping your head down and not getting into trouble is important!"

Miles looked at me with disbelief. "Keeping your head down is important? Like when you kept your head down when dad was cheating on us? Like that kind of important?"

The wind whistled behind my ears as the impact of Miles' words sunk in.

"Like keeping your head down when someone asks you if you have any real sons, like that kind of important? Keep your head down then too? You don't understand anything, Mom."

For the first time Miles' look of distain when he spoke to me didn't embarrass me, but infuriate me. "I don't understand? *I* don't understand? What exactly don't I understand?"

"It doesn't matter," Miles said, "if I'm good or not. It doesn't matter if I'm *respecting my teachers* or not, don't you get that? You always think, just put your head down, it'll be ok, just keep going, it'll all be ok. But some things are not ok. The world is fucked up, Mom, *fucked up*."

I stared at Miles, the rage leaving my body and entering his.

"Remember when we first moved here? When we baked those stupid cookies and walked all over the neighborhood passing them out?"

I nodded, slowly.

"Nobody does that. You told me people do that, but nobody does that. Has anyone ever come to *our* house and passed out cookies when they moved to our neighborhood?"

I shook my head.

"Remember my stupid Michael Jackson birthday party? The kids laughed about that for months afterwards. For *months*. They even talk about it now sometimes, remembering how dumb an idea it was."

"But you love Michael Jackson. What's wrong with that?"

"And remember that dentist? You bought me a lollipop afterwards as if that was all it took. As if the hurt of everyone laughing at us in the waiting area could be brushed away with an apple flavored blow-pop. But things can't just be brushed away." Miles made a sweeping motion along his exposed arm. "None of this can just be brushed away."

Miles turned from me and headed towards the car. I sought the words to defend myself, but I wasn't sure what the defense was. I wasn't even certain what I'd done wrong. Wasn't I supposed to give my son the birthday parties he wanted? Wasn't I supposed to try and protect him from racists and bullies? No mother is perfect. I knew I wasn't, but what was I supposed to have done differently in those instances, and what did Miles expect from me now?"

"What do you want me to do?" I asked. "What was I supposed to have done then?"

"*Not* keep your head down, that's for sure."

"Fight doesn't always make right, Miles."

"Silence certainly doesn't either."

Miles turned and fully faced me now that he'd reached the car. As we looked at each other the distance between us grew wider than ever. Not the color distance, necessarily, but the generational distance. I had been taught to fight for what was right, certainly, but with knitted blankets and $20 donations, not unwinnable rages against larger authority figures. My fight for justice involved a slow wearing away of the evil, like a steady drip of water on seemingly impenetrable marble. Miles clearly wanted to grab a sledgehammer.

Hunter was the one that started the fight," Miles said, "with the new kid, Owen. We tried to break it up. We were the *good* guys."

I walked towards the car. When I reached it, I paused before unlocking it. "I don't understand everything," I said, "you are right about that. But I do understand a lot. And I am always trying. The world is unfair Miles, you are right, but you still have to try your best. Picking fights all the time isn't your best, and it doesn't solve anything. I know that, at least. I have been living in this world longer than you, you know."

"We have not been living in the same world."

I sighed. "Let me ask you this. Why do you always have to get involved? Why can't you just let things go sometimes?"

Miles cupped his hands and blew on them to keep warm in the whipping wind. I suddenly wondered where his jacket was. "It isn't always up to me, Mom."

"Isn't it though?"

Miles stared at me. "No."

We stood there for a long moment, and then I unlocked the car and we went to McDonald's for lunch.

The way Cierra told the story to Bob, not only were Desmond and Miles the good guys, but it was Hunter and Josh that were the bad guys.

"They teased that poor kid, Owen, for weeks before it all got out of hand," Cierra said. "Those boys are trouble. They've never been anything but trouble. Do you know what they said to my son when we first moved here?" Cierra looked to Bob, then to me, then to Bob again. "They told him they already had their Black friend in the neighborhood, and they didn't need another."

Desmond coughed. "They were trying to be funny."

"Mmmhmm. I've seen those kids be cruel multiple times. Picking on anyone new, like Owen, or anyone overweight, like Michael, or anyone with a disability, like Landon. They're just terrible. I'm willing to bet they're behind this in some way."

My mind flew back to what I thought of as The Pool Incident. The summer before I'd been reading a book in a lounge chair by the neighborhood pool when a voice behind me had said, *It's cuz they're Black.* As I put my book down and lifted my head I'd heard a second voice reply, *Yeah, I can see that. You did say they dumb as shit.* I'd stood up then, toppling my water bottle and knocking my suntan lotion from the chair, and turned and made unflinching eye contact with Hunter. He'd held my gaze without the least embarrassment, while looking down on me from his six feet of height.

I didn't say anything, and with a smirk I'd let Hunter and his friends just walk away. Maybe Miles was right, I did keep my head down too much. But at the time I'd thought standing up itself was a statement, like I'd *said* something to those boys by my not remaining in my seat and keeping my head buried in my book.

"Cierra's right," I said to Bob. "Those kids are mean. They don't care about anyone. They're trouble."

"That may be," Bob acknowledged, "but the police don't have them in custody."

"Maybe they should," Cierra interjected.

But Bob shook his head. "The issue right now is what happened at that party. Miles told me there were other kids up on the second floor with him. He told me it wasn't him that attacked Sarah. That's why I want to know more about this girl Sarah. Why would she accuse Miles of rape if it didn't happen? Why would she say that?"

# Chapter 24

*I* got out my phone and stared at the picture on the home screen. It was old, and I hadn't replaced it even though Miles told me I should get a new wallpaper already, that it was embarrassing the photo of him I had there. But I ignored him and kept it. It was a selfie of Miles and I at the zoo, smiling in front of the Polar Bear exhibit while holding an extra-large bag of popcorn. The zoo had been one of our favorite places, and when he was little we'd gone to it too many times to count. Warm summer afternoons just the two of us, laughing in the car on the way over, talking while waiting in the exhibit to pet the stingrays, always eating at least one funnel cake and one bag of popcorn. Afternoons at the zoo could make me feel like I'd eased into motherhood, like into a stiff leather jacket that over time relaxes and molds to your frame. We hadn't been to the zoo in years, but I treasured the feeling it could still give me, and so I'd kept that picture up on my home screen despite the grief Miles gave me over how old it was.

I swiped away from it now, however, and opened my contacts folder, looking for Sarah's phone number. I knew it was hopeless. The only friend of Miles' I'd ever called was Desmond, and I'd only done that a couple of times. My finger pushed past an endless list of names, none of them anyone of importance, half of them people I couldn't even recall.

"Mrs. Z?"

I looked up as Desmond and Cierra approached.

"We're going home," Cierra said. "I need to feed Desmond, and we could both use a shower. But we'll be back. We'll bring you some food, and coffee too. You drink coffee, right?"

"Don't worry about it," I said, shaking my head. "That's kind of you to offer, but it's not necessary. Go home and rest. Get some sleep. I'm sure you're both exhausted."

Desmond and Cierra looked at each other, and when they started to protest I wondered myself why I was insisting they stay away. I could use them by my side, but I knew I would never admit it out loud.

"Really," I said, "there's no point in us all just waiting around here." And a few minutes later, they left.

Bob and I remained in the station, sitting next to each other, scrolling through our respective phones. I glanced at the partition at the front of the station and wondered if an officer would come out and yell at us for using our devices. Maybe you just couldn't use the recording feature inside the station, I thought, as we continued to scroll and no one emerged to reprimand us. I vaguely wondered if we were being left alone because we were white. I glanced at the woman with the large purse but her eyes were once again closed; she was either praying, or she'd fallen asleep.

When I got to the end of my contacts list I put the phone down and closed my own eyes. I hadn't been this tired since exam all-nighters in college, though even then, I don't think the exhaustion had felt this heavy. I wanted more than anything to curl up into a ball and rest in a comfortable place.

Instead, I gathered the bits of my strength together and opened my photos folder this time. I had hundreds of pictures in there, some more than a decade old. Miles stuffing his face with cake at an early birthday party. Miles building an arch at the Science Center, wearing his favorite Nike ballcap and black Spiderman t-shirt. Miles asleep with his head in my lap. As I scrolled I watched Miles age. Miles playing in the neighborhood with kids from the block. Miles walking to school with a smile on his face. Miles shooting hoops and looking athletic. I stopped at a picture of Miles and Desmond together on their bikes outside our apartment. I loved that picture. The best friends were leaning towards each other, carefree, both looking rather handsome. Staring at it, for the first time, I noticed a third figure in the background, hazy and out of focus. This person was standing half hidden behind a tree, their slim figure blending with the tree trunk well enough I'd not noticed their presence before. I squinted, and realized it was Sarah.

What had I been missing about their relationship all these years? I stared at the picture and felt a yawning gap between what I thought I knew of my son's life, and what probably was my son's life. When had that gap gotten so large and impenetrable? And then with a jolt I realized that I did have Sara's number, in a text message. She'd contacted me a year or so ago, looking for Miles. I hadn't thought much of it at the time, in part because Miles himself had dismissed it when I asked him about it later, but now it seemed prophetic. I opened my text messages and scrolled through the conversations until I found it.

*Hey Mrs. Z,*
*Sorry to bother you.*
*This is Sarah.*
*Is Miles there?*
*I need to talk to Miles.*

I read it three times. It didn't say much. But her sentences were complete. She used punctuation. She didn't call me dude. I had always liked Sarah, I admitted to myself. But then, I was no judge of character.

"Here," I said, holding the phone out to Bob. "I found Sarah's number."

"Call her," he said, pushing my arm back towards me. "Find out exactly what she said to the police." At my hesitation

Bob continued, "You know her. She's more likely to trust you than me."

"Ok," I reluctantly agreed. I stood up, and after gathering some strength and courage about me, stepped outside to make the call.

The cool, early dawn air enveloped me in an embrace as the door to the station clicked shut behind me. There was a bit of light outside now and I blinked into it, rubbing my eyes and face with both hands. I took my phone out of my pocket and saw that it was 6:53 a.m., nearly five hours since I'd first gotten the call from Miles. It felt like a lifetime, and yet, not long enough. I wished time would pass so this awful episode could be packed away and put behind us and we could return to our life together back at the apartment. But at the same time, I didn't actually know how this would end, so I knew I needed to appreciate this suspended moment before, god help us, everything about our simple, easy life was over.

I stared at Sarah's text message. What was the worst that could happen, I thought, that she wouldn't answer my call? No, the worst that could happen was that she'd hang up on me. No, I thought again, the worst that could happen, of course, was that she'd repeat the accusation of rape. And I couldn't countenance that, I just couldn't. My hand shook as I pressed dial on the phone.

I'd lost the trust of my own mother once. When I was sixteen years old, the same age as Miles was now. I'd been asked out on a date by a boy two years older than me and ten inches taller. I hadn't even realized he'd known who I was, this mature upperclassman with the silky brown hair, and I'd felt flattered, if also overwhelmed, when he'd asked me out.

He'd driven up to our house on a Saturday evening in a battered, blue Chevy Nova, and I'd run out to meet him, hoping to avoid my mother interacting with him on our doorstep. I'd urged him out of the driveway before she could put her shoes on and come out to speak to us, and I'd felt a win at the successful evasion. Steve and I hadn't returned until two in the morning, and when I turned my key in the lock of our front door at that late hour, my mother had swung it open apoplectic with rage. *Where have you been? What have you been doing? You are* so *grounded.*

My mother stared at me, and I at her.

*What if you're pregnant?*

At the time, I'd laughed, and she'd grounded me for a full three months, the longest I'd ever been grounded in my life. When my mother finally spoke to me again, weeks later, I explained to her that Steve's battery had died when we'd left the lights on parked in the Taco Bell parking lot. All we'd done was talk in his car, for hours, until someone had come along and given us a jump. When I'd finished explaining things, my mother had looked at me, and finally blinked.

It dawned on me only then how stupid it had been of me not to have known how upset she would be at my coming home so late. I thought once I'd explained what had happened, she'd be fine with it. But I realized with an embarrassed clarity how traumatic the wait had been for her that night. Months later, my mother shared with me her own story of a violent episode with a boy when she was eighteen, of her escape, of her years of lingering fear. Like the lengthening ripples of a disturbed pond, I had felt the tentacles of history reach out and grip us both.

Miles was like me, I thought. He might do thoughtless things because he was young, he might upset me, argue with me, chafe under some of my rules, but he loved me, and I knew that he hated disappointing me. He would never violate my trust. This was all a misunderstanding, I knew it, just as my first night out with a boy had been a misunderstanding so many years before.

I listened to the ring on the phone and braced myself for the possibility that Sarah would repeat her accusation. If she did, I knew I would still maintain a faith in my son. Whatever Sarah said, there would still be his side of the story too. I had to hear it all, however, to know what to do.

"He-llo?" The voice at the other end of the line was nebulous, soft. It could disappear in an instant.

"Sarah? Is that you? This is Miles' mom. We need to talk."

For a long minute there was silence. And then, I heard crying.

A wave of emotion flooded over me. Pity, for this poor girl who was clearly suffering. Confusion, as I didn't know whether to comfort her, or interrogate her. Worry, that I was betraying my boy by having empathy for his accuser. Exhaustion, from the strain of it all.

"Sarah," I pressed, "I need to understand what happened."

She mumbled something, but I didn't catch it.

"What? I didn't hear you."

Sarah blew her nose and took a deep breath. "I'm sorry, Mrs. Z. I tried to tell them. I told them it wasn't Miles. But they wouldn't listen to me. They've got the wrong guy."

# Chapter 25

*S*arah was in no condition to talk on the phone for long, but before she hung up, I found out more of what had happened.

The kids were calling it TAD, as in, *you going to TAD?* Or, *have you heard about this weekend's TAD Party?* It was the middle of November, ThAnksgiving Day was around the corner, and the kids were all offering up thanks somebody's parents had been trusting enough, or stupid enough, to leave town before the holiday. The festivities had started at midday on Friday, with kids coming and going, first bringing beer, then hard liquor, then drugs including pot and meth. According to Sarah, most of the entire high school had shown up to the party at some point, although not Desmond and Miles. She confirmed what I thought I knew about my son and his best friend, that they both shunned the big house parties. Sarah let me know that she always noticed their absence, too. She said that everyone noticed their absence, and wondered what kind of parties they went to, if the local ones weren't good enough for them. Everyone was certain Desmond and Miles partied *somewhere,* if not in the neighborhood.

"I, I was really hoping Miles would come to the party," Sarah admitted.

"Why?"

"I like Miles. He's a friend. And Miles and Desmond have a way about them. They're quiet when all the other boys are loud. They're steady, when the jocs are impulsive. They always seem so strong and sure of themselves, like they know what they're doing. I think most of the other boys are afraid of them."

I was surprised to hear this. Neither Miles nor Desmond was especially tall, or big, or imposing in any way. But they were Black. And they could stand quietly. I guess that was all it took.

"You know," Sarah's voice dropped even lower than it already was, as if she were about to tell me a secret, "Miles has always been there for me. In middle school kids used to pick on me for dressing like a tomboy, for wearing those ridiculous boots I had all the time and never brushing my hair, but not Miles. Miles always stuck up for me."

"I didn't know that."

"I know he has a crush on me," Sarah continued, "I'm not dumb. And I don't like him like that, so I don't always return his texts or answer his calls. But I've always liked him. I've always liked him a lot." I waited and, after a pause, Sarah went on. "I never wanted anything bad to happen to him. You've got to know that."

Her words made me anxious. "So what happened?"

"It was late. After midnight, I think. I don't know, but it was dark outside and I'd been at the party for hours at that point. I was tired, of all the drinking and drugs, and I just wanted to go home. It was past my curfew anyway and I really needed to get home, but, I couldn't leave," Sarah sounded defensive, as if I'd asked her why she hadn't. "I'd told my friend Olivia I wouldn't leave without her, and she'd disappeared. I didn't know where she was. I looked all over, but I couldn't find her." Sarah sounded desperate, as if worried all over again for her friend. "I searched outside, inside, and then I went upstairs to look for her, in the bedrooms. I was so tired." Sarah's voice drifted away. "I realize now that what I did was dumb. I'm so sorry. I wasn't thinking." Sarah started to cry again and I didn't know what to do. I couldn't follow what she was saying anymore.

"What was dumb?" I asked. "What did you do?"

"I went into one of the bedrooms and laid down. I was so tired," she repeated. "I fell asleep. Although, I'm not sure I actually fell asleep, or if I was just in that groggy, almost-sleep place. Either way, I was laying down when someone came into the room." Sarah was quiet for a minute. "It felt distant though, as if from far away. As if I might be dreaming. I heard rustling sounds. I thought it might be Olivia, so I opened my eyes." Sarah's voice caught, but she continued. "And, and he was already standing over me, with, with his pants down." Sarah burst into tears and had a hard time continuing.

"It's all my fault," she stammered. "I, I never should have gone into that room."

I felt a wave of pity for Sarah. I remembered high school parties and the pressures sometimes felt at them. My big mistake had been to get so drunk once I threw up in a friend's living room, and then, embarrassed, grabbed a stranger's car keys and tried to drive home. It hadn't been my best moment.

"It's not your fault," I told Sarah. I was offering succor to a girl I still wasn't sure hadn't improperly reported my son to the police. I felt for her, but at the same time, I was getting anxious to hear the rest of the story.

"You told the police it was Miles in the room?" I asked Sarah.

"No," she said, her tears drying up. "They never asked me, actually, though I tried to tell them that."

"So you *didn't* report a rape?"

"Well no, I did, I had to, they were there, but it wasn't Miles. I never said it was Miles. It was— It was—, Hunter." Her voice had grown tremulous again. "He was the one who—, the one who—, the one who did it."

I was confused. "Then how did Miles get blamed?" I asked, a bit too harshly. How had my son gotten in the middle of this?

"I— I'd had my phone with me on the bed," Sarah said. "I called Miles before Hunter pinned me down. I hadn't meant to, I was just pressing anything, any number, trying to call anyone. I think Miles picked up and he heard us struggling. He may have heard me beg for help."

My poor boy. What an awful call to receive. I could imagine the expression on Miles' face as it dawned on him what was going on. I'm sure he was horrified. That was when he must have ordered Desmond to turn around and drive straight to the party.

Sarah cried for a few minutes, and I didn't interrupt her grief. "He tried to save me," she finally said through her tears. "Hunter had barred the door with a chair so no one could get in, but when Miles got there he forced his way in. He tried to save me. He was the only one who tried to save me." I could tell from the way Sarah's voice trailed off, however, that Miles hadn't come in time.

"Olivia was the one who called the police," Sarah continued. "She'd finally come looking for me, and heard me crying behind the door. She'd been the first to try and get in, but when she couldn't, she called the police. It was after her call and before the police showed up that Miles got there. Miles broke the door down, and had just punched Hunter when the police arrived. They found the two of them fighting," Sarah told me, taking a deep, ragged breath. "I was huddled with Olivia on a corner of the bed while Miles and Hunter fought."

Sarah didn't have to keep talking for me to imagine the rest. The police showed up, barged into the bedroom, mistook Miles for the rapist and Hunter for the savior, threw Miles to the ground, told him to shut up, and handcuffed him. Ignoring pleas from Sarah and everyone else in the room, adrenaline racing, music playing, smoke swirling, voices loud, confusion louder, the police had drawn their guns. They had pointed them at the kids.

I knew I should be grateful that Miles had escaped with his life.

# Chapter 26

***O***ver the next hour, as morning dawned and the sun filtered its desultory way through the windows of the police station, things picked up. The woman with the large purse who'd sat across from me for most of the night, and who seemed like something of a friend by morning, was called up to the partition and completed some paperwork. When she was done she disappeared into the back of the station. An older man needing to pay a parking ticket came in, did so, and then stumbled back out. A pair of middle-aged men entered the station, had a conversation with a group of police officers that came out to greet them, and then left with smiles and purposeful strides. My lawyer and I seemed to be the only interminable constants. We sat in our chairs, talking little, waiting.

I had assumed that the conversation with Sarah was enough to get Miles out. I was elated when the call ended, thinking that I'd just solved the case, that Bob would congratulate me and slap me on the back, and that we'd walk up to the front desk and finish this thing already. The overwhelming weight on my shoulders had lifted momentarily and I'd felt I could breathe again. I couldn't understand, at first, why Bob wasn't as excited as I was.

"She needs to tell it to the police," he told me.

"She tried. When they first showed up. But there was too much commotion at the party. The police wouldn't listen."

"It sounds like she only told you."

I stared at Bob, open-mouthed.

"Did she go to the hospital? Did she complete a rape kit?"

"I— I don't know." Anger rose from deep within me. "I told you to call her, not me. Obviously, I didn't know what I was supposed to ask her."

"It's ok," Bob said, relenting a little. He reached out a hand to touch me. "Just call her again. Ask if she had a rape kit done. That will be valuable evidence, if Miles is innocent."

"*If* Miles is innocent? Did you really just say *if* Miles is innocent?"

"You know what I mean," Bob said, trying to smile. "Just call her."

When I didn't move Bob tried again. "You did a good job, no, you did a great job speaking with the girl. We just need her to talk to the police now, ok?"

I turned angrily from the lawyer and got out my phone. But when I dialed Sarah's number, it went straight to voicemail. I was shaking by the time I put the phone back in my pocket.

Bob looked at me, then at the front desk, then back at me. He seemed to decide something. "Let me talk to them," he said, getting up.

While Bob spoke to an officer I tried Sarah's number a few more times, but she was no longer answering. I looked across the station, out the window, and into the distance, and felt more alone than I ever had in my life. I needed connections. If I knew the police chief, or was friends with an alderman, say, none of this would be happening. I would just make a well-placed phone call, promise someone a favor, and get my son released. It was all about who you knew, and where you could put pressure, and I had never been big enough to exert any kind of pressure on anyone.

My next thought was to get the media involved, but I wasn't certain how one did such a thing. Did you call a newsroom and ask to speak to a reporter? But it was early on a

Saturday morning, what newsroom would be open? I hesitated also because I doubted anyone would care. This wasn't a murder, no celebrities were involved, it was just a story about a bunch of high school kids at a house party. So predictable. So cliché. Just another girl being raped.

I racked my brains, but I couldn't think of anything I could do for my son. I had thought it would take longer than this. I had thought it wouldn't be until he was a grown adult, with kids and a mortgage, that I'd become superfluous to his life. I'd always pictured myself calling him when he was older and offering parenting advice, and my son only pretending to listen to me, but loving me just the same. I imagined him and his kids helping me, as my hair grew white and my hips gave out, and I stumbled around with a cane. I never imagined I'd be of no help to him before he'd even left the house, while he was still in high school, when he was only sixteen years old. He wasn't even a man yet, yet he was facing a man's problems.

I consoled myself with the thought that at least the truth was on our side. Sarah's testimony, the rape kit evidence if there was any, other witnesses in the room like Olivia. They couldn't keep my son for long, not with so much pointing to his innocence. It wouldn't make any sense to do so. But then I remembered the Central Park Five, James Tillman, Ryan Ferguson, Dontre Hamilton, Sandra Bland, Eric Garner, and Tamir Rice, and I knew that truth, eye-witnesses, and evidence didn't matter; they could all crumble before a determined, prejudiced authority. The narrative was what mattered, and my outcast Black son as the evil rapist of an innocent white girl was a familiar narrative the police, and the public, could get behind.

# Chapter 27

***T**endrils of hair whipped across my face as the wind outside blew past. I saw that the early morning traffic on the overpass in the distance had picked up considerably. I'd stepped outside to clear my head and think. There had to be something I could do. I wasn't perfect. I'd made mistakes as a mother, god knows, from buying the wrong sized diapers and light-toned band aids, to leaving Miles unattended in the kitchen and letting him watch Nate and I fight, but I'd also done some things right, like encourage his love of music, surround him with books, and talk to him about everything from Juneteenth to July 4th.

When Miles was little and still liked to grocery shop with me, I'd sometimes tell him as we walked up and down the aisles, he in the front of the cart, me pushing it along, that he was my most expensive purchase. My son would sit taller, and smile wider, thinking about how precious an item he was. When we got home and were putting away the groceries, he'd turn to me and ask, *How expensive was I?* I would open my empty wallet, tip it over, and say, *you were worth all the money in the world.* Miles grew up thinking he was more precious than diamonds, and he was right.

As Miles got older and we increasingly fought over everything from schoolwork to laundry, he sometimes threw at me

*You're not my real mother.* Even the first time he said it, however, it didn't faze me much. Because what kid didn't identify with Harry Potter or Oliver Twist or Cinderella or Naruto? I wasn't adopted and I could remember imagining a different life for myself, a better life, one with a kinder mother that didn't make me do the dishes. *No,* I would say to Miles, hugging him despite his squirming protests, *but I am the mother that's here.*

I let my fingers brush over the minifigure now in my pocket, and imagined holding my son again. I could feel his presence around me, his arms encircling my arms, his back bending towards me, his chapped lips brushing my cheek. It was uncanny how well a mother knew her own child's body, the mole on the upper left side of his shoulder, the scar on his right thigh, the long, ticklish toes. Such knowledge was earned from hours spent comforting a child, first as a baby in the middle of the night, then as a toddler sick with fever, later as a boy scared by the dark. Even as a teenager, side-by-side on the couch, watching TikTok videos together.

A shock of awareness passed through me. I felt a chill, and then a spreading warmth. I suddenly knew how to get Miles out of jail.

I called Desmond and he answered right away. "I'm not sure," he said, sounding more hesitant than I'd hoped. "But I can give you a few numbers to call."

I wrote down the phone numbers he rattled off to me on a notepad I found in my car, and started calling them the minute we hung up.

At first, no one could help me. I began to deflate when one kid after another either didn't answer my call, or said they couldn't help me. Most were sympathetic, however, and though they didn't have much to offer, they told me to keep calling and not give up. Almost everyone gave me other numbers to call. I kept at it, dialing number after number, refusing to believe this wasn't going to work. I wouldn't give up, not until I'd called the entire high school if I had to.

And then, I got lucky.

A boy named Ethan with a surprisingly deep voice answered the phone like it wasn't eight in the morning on a weekend and told me that yeah, he had had his phone out, and yeah, he had been there when it happened, and yeah, he had recorded the whole thing. I didn't know this kid Ethan, I couldn't picture him at all, though I knew most of the kids at Miles' school. His answers to my questions were short, his voice betrayed little empathy, but he agreed to share his recording with me, and that was all that mattered. He sent me the file as soon as we hung up.

My hands were sweating so much by the time the recording came in, I had a hard time opening it. I'd had to use both hands to grip the phone and keep it from slipping away. I watched the video and saw, quite clearly, Miles *outside* the bedroom door, trying to get in. Sarah's cries for help could be heard in the background. The shaky recording showed my son jamming his shoulder against the door, working to break it down. It showed Miles falling inside, Hunter and Sarah in a jumble on the bed. It proved things had happened just as Sarah had described — Miles confronting Hunter, and the fight that ensued.

Not bothering with the lawyer, I strode into the police station, walked right up to the front desk, and banged on the plastic partition with the strength of Thor wielding his hammer. The startled officer on the other side stared at me. "I have proof," I said in a too-loud voice that, distantly, I realized sounded somewhat hysterical. "I have a video of my son *outside* the bedroom, trying to get in, not inside doing anything wrong. I have proof of him saving the girl, not hurting her. You have to listen to me. I am his mother and I have proof."

# Chapter 28

*T*he blond-haired, blue-eyed police officer tilted his head to the side, and then decided it was worth the effort to get up and speak to me. I watched with satisfaction as he hoisted himself up from behind the desk and came around to the partition where I was standing. I was aware of Bob approaching me from behind.

"Let me see it first," Bob whispered in my ear.

But I swatted him away.

"Look," I said, angling the phone towards the officer and playing the video. The sound of Miles banging down the door reverberated around us.

I had a flashback of Miles and I at home, watching a crime show together, a similar sound emanating from the television. Miles and I would be back together side-by-side on the couch again soon, I told myself. It had to happen now.

The officer glanced at me when the video ended, but didn't say anything. His visage reminded me of my co-workers at the bank — superior, aloof, annoyed by my mere presence. After a moment, however, he turned, and headed into the back of the station.

"Give me the phone," Bob said, in an authoritative voice I hadn't thought he'd earned. I handed it to him and he watched the video a few more times. I imagined the look on Miles' face when he learned that he was being released; the relief that would spill down his body like a shower. I thought about the meal I would cook him when we got home – chicken pot pie, his favorite, or no, maybe something simpler for the moment but still comforting, like burritos. I pictured us sitting at the kitchen table, eating. That was all I wanted to do in the world. Make my son a homecooked meal and watch him eat it.

"Do you know the other kids in this video?" Bob asked. "It will help if the police decide to keep pressing this."

"What is there to press?" After the phone call with Sarah, and now this video of the actual incident, how could there by anything left to prove? I was incredulous at just the thought.

"Videos can be doctored," Bob said, "I've seen it before."

"But—" I stuttered, "who would even do that?"

The blond officer returned along with two other tall men in uniform, interrupting our conversation. The video was played again. And then, yet again. The battery was running low on my phone and I felt mild panic that it would run out before the officers were convinced.

"Where did you get this?" one of them asked.

"From someone who was there, clearly."

"The girl is willing to testify that it wasn't Miles Zame," Bob added. "She never identified Miles as the rapist."

The officers huddled together a few steps away from us, but I couldn't imagine what more they needed to discuss to let my son go. I leaned in their direction, trying to overhear what they were saying.

"It won't look good," Bob called out, "to keep an innocent boy locked up for much longer."

Twenty minutes later there was a loud click and I realized with a jolt that the side detention door was about to open. In a moment someone, hopefully Miles, would walk out. I stood up and willed the person behind the door to be my son. My knees buckled but I caught myself, and steadied myself.

When the door at last swung open my eyes indeed rested on my son, standing in his favorite sneakers and jeans, the gray

Nike sweatshirt I'd bought him last Christmas. My breath caught at the sight of him and for a brief moment I felt the core of my body step outside itself, and then shatter. Shards of emotion hurtled in all directions: love, fear, exhaustion, hope, joy, disbelief. It was the same powerful feeling I'd had sixteen years before, when I'd first glimpsed Miles as a baby in the hospital. And in the space that was created by the bursting of my heart, love bloomed. I knew then, as I knew now, that my life had unalterably pivoted.

I rushed towards Miles and wrapped my arms around him. "You're ok," I said. "You're free." I inhaled familiar scents from his childhood, boy sweat, hot breath, the sharp tang of adrenaline. "You're ok," I repeated, realizing how wooden he felt, how little he was hugging me back. "It's over."

Miles pulled away and rubbed his eyes. I gave him some space. He didn't move forward, however, he just stood where he was. I tried to urge him across the threshold but he seemed rooted to the spot, stuck on the precipice between confinement and freedom, between the past and the future, between injustice and justice.

"What's wrong?" I asked.

Miles shook his head. "I—" he turned to me then, sorrow stamping his handsome features. "I'm sorry. Mom, I—" His breath caught, but he recovered it. "Can you forgive me? You always told me to be careful, and I wasn't. I should have listened to you better. You were right, Mom. Keep your head down. I'm sorry."

A wave of shock passed through me. Why was Miles asking for *my* forgiveness? I'd been wondering this entire time how I was going to apologize to him, how I was going to ask his forgiveness for all I'd done wrong over the years, for all I didn't know, for all I couldn't help with, but here he was saying the words first. "What for?" was all I could think to say.

"For everything," Miles said. Despite his near six feet of height, my son suddenly looked like the babe I knew him to be.

I shook my head. "No, Miles. *I'm* sorry. Can you forgive *me*? For not protecting you better. For not getting you out of here sooner." I held my son's face in my hands. "You helped someone in need," I told him, "regardless of the consequences. That's what a hero does. You have nothing to apologize for."

But Miles' gaze wasn't on me. He was looking down, at the ground, still not moving forward.

"Don't apologize for other people's mistakes. There's no need to apologize to me, or anyone else for that matter, for doing the right thing, for being who you are." I wrapped my arms around Miles again. "My precious child," I whispered in his ear, "worth all the money in the world."

My son held me close then and we stood there, Black arms intertwined with white arms. Mother, holding up son. Son, holding up mother. And for just a moment, time stood still.

I kissed Miles on the cheek. He was safe, for now. Miles was my baby, and I would take care of him until the very last breath was taken from my body. I no longer cared what anyone, anywhere, any color said about it. Miles was my treasure, my love, my greatest joy. He was my reason for being. He was my son. And the two of us were finally going home, together.

**Lea Rachel** is the author of *The Other Shakespeare* and other works of fiction and non-fiction. Originally from Detroit, Michigan, she now lives in St. Louis, MO with her husband and son, and teaches at the University of Missouri, St. Louis.

You can find out more about Lea, including other writing projects, at www.learachel.com.